MURDER BY
CANDLELIGHT

BLYTHE BAKER

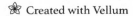 Created with Vellum

～

A dramatic death...

When an evening's entertainment unexpectedly turns into a night of death, Alice Beckingham must discover the motive behind a very public murder. But with hundreds of witnesses, narrowing down her suspects isn't easy. Worse, her investigation makes Alice a target for a killer who doesn't want to be caught.

With the always aloof Sherborne Sharp assisting, can Alice stay alive long enough to solve the puzzle? Or will the next curtain rise on yet another murder – her own?

～

Dearest Alice,

    Excuse the hastiness of this letter, but I'm writing this only minutes before Achilles and I leave for a short work trip to Los Angeles. We have a new client there we are to meet with, but I could not delay responding to your questions until our return.

    I know you do not take kindly to orders or commands, but I implore you not to look into the matter of *The Chess Master* any further. Truly, even writing his name leaves me with a chill down my spine. There are some people who do not deserve our time or attention, and *The Chess Master* is one of the foremost in that category. He was a cruel man who did cruel things and for little to no reason. Unfortunately, your brother Edward found himself entangled in that dark man's hold and it cost him his life. Following the same path he took, trying to find reason in crimes and deeds that are unreasonable, will only hurt you. At best, you will become wise to the darkest parts of this world, the corners that I hope you never have to see.

I do not tell you any of this because I do not think you can handle it, but because you should not have to. If it will keep you from inquiring any further, I will quickly tell you my own tale.

I came into contact with The Chess Master on several occasions. The first time being just prior to that horrible weekend at the family estate in Somerset. He warned me of the crime that would occur, though I did not understand his meaning at the time. Later, as I investigated further, I realized that The Chess Master had been behind Edward's crime. It may have very well been your brother's idea to kill your sister's suitor, but he was encouraged in the idea by The Chess Master. Once Edward's crimes were discovered and he was arrested, I believe The Chess Master grew nervous that he would say too much. As a man who lived only in the shadows, he did not want any light to be shined on his existence. So, he had your brother murdered in prison. I am sorry to deliver this news to you, but I hope it is some consolation that several years ago now, I have it on good authority that The Chess Master fell off of a bridge into the Thames. He was then run over by a boat.

Again, I am sorry to deliver the news, and I hope you will not be offended by my request that you do not look into the matter further. I know you are a grown woman now and will do as you please. I only hope it will please you to lead a normal life far from such gruesome matters as crime and murder.

Achilles is requesting I wrap up this letter, so I will write again when we return home. I do not know when that will be, but I look forward to speaking with you.

I love you dearly, Alice, and wish only health and happiness for you.

Love,

Rose

I TUCKED the letter back into its envelope and slid it into the top drawer of my writing desk, knowing full well I would retrieve it again before the day was out. I'd read the message twelve times since it arrived a week ago, hoping with each reread that more information would present itself to me. That some secret code written into the body of the letter would reveal itself, and I would know more than I currently did.

It was good to finally hear it confirmed that Edward's death in prison had been a murder. If nothing else, that was one mystery solved. The other mystery remained, however: who was The Chess Master?

Rose said she was in contact with him—or he with her, actually, since he sent her the first piece of correspondence—but she did not say who the man was. She said that he fell into the Thames, but she did not say that he died. For every piece of information my cousin offered, she withheld something vital.

I had answered her letter immediately, though I knew she would not receive it or read it until she returned from Los Angeles, and I had sent her several letters still with more questions that I could not keep inside my head any longer.

What is The Chess Master's true identity? Did he die after his fall into the Thames? Why would he reach out to you if the two of you had never previously met? If his connection was to Edward, why would he not contact Catherine or me first, rather than you? If he did die, why did news of the discovery of his body not reach the newspapers or the police?

I wrote so many letters that my mother grew suspicious. Her first thought was that I wanted to move to San Francisco with Rose and Achilles and was trying to arrange the matter with Rose via letter. Now that she had lost a son and her eldest daughter had moved away, my mother existed in a perpetual kind of fear that I would leave, as well. She tried to feign support for any decision I made, but I could tell she wanted to keep me close.

She had seemed comforted when I assured her I had no intentions of moving, though she shouldn't have been. If she knew I was looking into my brother's death, she would be beside herself. She and my father had spent the years since his death trying to distance our family from his misdeeds, and we had only very recently succeeded. Mama and Papa were being invited to social events at a similar frequency to before the crime and subsequent death, and life seemed, as much as possible, as though it was returning to normal. I could not be the one to steal that illusion from my parents.

I lay back on my bed and took a deep breath. I tried to ignore the muffled sounds of London traffic outside my window and the nearer whispers of gentle movement in the hall outside my bedroom, most likely a servant tidying up or fetching something for my mother. I focused inward, trying to form a plan of what to do next.

I considered writing another letter to Catherine. My sister had been the one to inform me of the existence of The Chess Master in the first place, since I'd been too young at the time of the crimes to hear any of the information firsthand. However, after my last letter, she had made it quite clear that she had no interest in thinking about our brother's actions or The Chess Master. She was more than a little preoccupied with other matters in her life, and she did not have the innate curiosity I'd been born with. If a thing did not trouble Catherine directly then it did not take up any space in her head. I was not as lucky. Still, I did not want to be the person to distress her with questions she likely wouldn't have the answers to, anyway.

Going to my parents with my questions was not an option, of course. I had no idea what they knew of Edward's death, and I did not want to be the person to reopen that wound if they were content with the answers the authorities had supplied us. Truly, I wished I could be content. I wished my brain did not race to theories and possibilities. It would be nice to feel at ease for once. To not look over my shoulder as I walked down the street.

Even when Mama, Papa, and I had gone to visit Catherine in Yorkshire recently, I had imagined a shadowy figure was lurking around the corner of Catherine's house, waiting like a tiger to pounce on my family when we least expected it. I snuck away from the happy reunion to surprise the person and demand to know why he was watching us, only to frighten a gardener half to death. The man was tending to the flowers and gripped his chest as though having an attack. The entire incident made Catherine so cross she wouldn't speak to me for the better part of the day.

Even now that the visit had ended and I was back in London, I was not at ease. More than anything, Rose's letter left me with the uncomfortable feeling that she was leaving something out. Rose clearly had many of her own secrets. She had allowed me access to many of them, but out of respect for her, I had decided years ago not to push her farther than she was willing to go. Now, though, I wanted to push her. I wanted to drag the information from her simply because I believed that information had more to do with me than Rose was willing to admit, perhaps even to herself.

Even more, I wondered if The Chess Master might still be alive.

It was quite possible my paranoia had rattled my brain, but I didn't think so. If Rose knew the man to be dead, she would have said so plainly. Yet, she skirted around the matter. She said enough that any reasonable person would assume he was dead—he had fallen from a bridge and been run over, after all—but as Rose well knew, I had never been a reasonable person. Unless someone had pressed their fingers to the pulse of the criminal mastermind, I would not accept him as dead.

I lifted myself from the bed, wrapped my robe around my waist, and walked back to the desk. My fingers dragged across the smooth wood of my desk, itching to pull out the letter and reread it again, even though I knew nothing more would come from it.

Finally, I balled my hands into fists and crawled under the blankets to try and rest. Reading the letter again would be a waste of time and would only frustrate me. So, I came to a decision then and there.

If I could not go to Catherine or my parents, and Rose's responses would be similarly unhelpful, then, despite Rose's warning, I simply had to investigate the matter myself. Rose had really given me no other choice.

2

"We leave in half an hour," my mother said, her voice chasing me up the stairs. "Do not be late."

"There would have been no danger of that if you had informed me of the event earlier in the day," I called back.

My mother said nothing because she knew I was right. She'd waited until dinner to inform me that she and my father were going to attend a theatre performance at The Royal Coliseum, and I would be welcome to join them. She said it as though they had just decided to go, but I knew for a fact they'd been invited by the owner the weekend before because my father mentioned it when they returned from dinner at Mr. Williamson's home.

The truth of it was that my parents had been out of the house every night save one for the last two weeks, and my mother felt badly for leaving me out.

I could not care less, of course. The years after

Edward's crime and death have been long ones for our family. Long, quiet stretches of grief dotted with moments of hope. As time has gone on, those hopeful moments have grown brighter and more lasting. Moments turned to days and weeks and months where things could almost feel normal again. So, I could not find the energy to be upset at sitting home alone when I was too busy being happy that my parents were acting like themselves again.

Though, I also would not turn down an invitation to the theatre. As a child, it had been my least favorite place to go. Hours spent sitting in an uncomfortable seat in a crowded room, trying to pay attention to a story I didn't understand the nuances of. Like many things, my appreciation of theatre came with maturity. Now, I found it a magical escape.

Longer dresses had come back into fashion, which would work well for me. I usually froze half to death in the theatre, and at least this way, my legs would be covered to the ankle once seated. I selected a deep red gown from the front of my closet. I'd bought it just the week before when out on a shopping trip with my friend, Virginia Williams. She selected the dress for me, claiming it would go perfectly with the warm tones in my hair and eyes. I trusted her opinion wholly since she was very close to finishing up her education in fashion with the hopes of one day being a buyer for a department store.

As soon as I put on the dress, I knew I'd made the right decision.

It draped down to my ankles in ruffled layers with flowing lace sleeves that reached to my elbows. A bow with long, hanging ends hung from the waist to near my knee, cinching the dress in slightly, and fabric flowers were pinned to the neckline.

Since I didn't have long to get ready, I opted for a gold headband to hold my short hair in place, hopefully hiding some of the places where the curls had begun to fall. Then, I dabbed blush onto the rounds of my cheeks, added a swirl of dark liner around my eyes, and finished the look with a red lipstick the same shade as my gown. Papa would disapprove of the makeup, but he never approved of anything that made me look my age. If he had his way, I'd wear my hair in long boring braids and trade all of my sleek gowns in for the frilly dresses of my youth.

When I met my parents in the entryway, I could see the disapproval on my father's face at once. Mama, however, beamed.

"You are going to be the most beautiful woman in the room," she said, grabbing my hands and spinning me around.

"That will be hard when you are there." I winked.

She rolled her eyes and batted away the compliment. "I'm an old woman now. You are young and gorgeous. Isn't she gorgeous, James?"

"Lovely," he said, glancing at his watch. "We should go. George is waiting."

George, the chauffeur, stood on the curb next to the car, his hands folded in front of him. He tipped his head as we approached, and opened the door to the back seat. "Good evening, Lord and Lady Ashton. Miss Beckingham."

"George," my father replied absently.

I was the last person into the car, and George gave me a small smile. For years, I had treated George as a kind of convenience in my life. Ever-present and occasionally useful, though not especially noteworthy. That was until he'd recently become a confidante for my investigations. Not only did George offer me a great deal of help, but I learned that he was a thoughtful, gentle man who cared about my family a great deal more than I ever knew.

"Nice to see you, George," I said, tipping my head.

The ride to the theatre was quick, urged on by my father's increasing insistence that we would be late if we did not hurry.

"Are you trying to push the car to its limits?" my mother asked. "George is getting us there as quickly as he can, James."

"I just do not want to walk in halfway through the first act. If that is the case, it is better to not attend at all."

She patted my father's leg. "We won't be late."

Mama was right. When we arrived, many well-dressed people were still standing outside in the chilly evening, talking and greeting one another. We passed by them into the lobby where even more people filled the golden, glowing space.

The ceilings were tall, accentuated by a golden dome in the center that capped the beautiful entrance hall like a halo.

We checked our coats and bags, and then my parents began greeting the numerous people they knew in the crowd. Long-time friends, business associates, and heads of committees Mama organized shook their hands, remarked on what a beautiful young lady I'd grown to be, and then talked of their excitement for the show.

The gentlemen all seemed to remark on the numbers.

"Twenty cast and even more crew," one man said, white eyebrows raised. "Not to mention the sets they have to unpack. It is a wonder touring theatre performances happen at all."

"This is their twenty-seventh show this year," another said.

My father nodded. "According to the paper, they'll be here for ten days before moving on to the next. What an exhausting lifestyle."

The ladies cared nothing for the facts and spoke only of the lead actor, Phineas St. Clair.

"I don't care how young he is," my mother's dear friend, Margaret Blackwell, said. "That Phineas St. Clair is one handsome face."

"You aren't thinking of leaving me now, are you, Madge?" her husband asked, taking her appreciation of the much younger man in stride.

"Of course not," she said, wrapping her arm around his and patting his elbow. "I made a vow for life, so I will wait until after the funeral, at least, before I put myself back on the market."

The group laughed at the naughty joke, but I couldn't help myself from staring at Madge's husband. The joke seemed especially distasteful since he looked to be close to death already. That funeral might not be far off.

"Besides, I read that St. Clair has been romantically linked to the lead actress," my mother added. "What is her name? Rosalie something, I believe."

"Rosalie Stuart," I said, holding up the program with the woman's name printed squarely across the front.

"That was in a gossip column, but I haven't seen it

proven," Madge said. "Until I do, I'll continue my dreaming. Phineas St. Clair is a vision."

I did have to agree that Phineas St. Clair made a rather lovely picture. Large posters of him hung like tapestries on either side of the tall wooden doors into the theatre. He was poised under a spotlight with one hand wrapped around his female co-star, the other tucked behind his back and holding a gun.

"What is the play about anyway?" I asked, gesturing to the poster.

"You came without knowing what you'd come to see?" Madge asked.

I shrugged and then frowned playfully at my mother. "I didn't know I'd be coming at all until an hour ago."

"Well, you look lovely for such late notice," Madge said, admiring my gown. Then, she leaned in, excited to share the details of the play she had already memorized. "I read all about it in the paper along with a list of glowing reviews as long as my arm. Everyone loves it."

"Tell the girl what it is about," her husband said, releasing a wheezy cough at the end that made me worried he really would die soon.

She shushed her husband. "Phineas St. Clair plays the husband, and he and his wife are grifters. They lied and connived their way into the upper echelons of society, but when they are found out by a peer, Phineas St. Clair kills the man to keep their secret. The paper remained vague so as not to ruin the ending, but they have to work hard to cover the murder and it strains their marriage. My theory is that he will end up killing the wife to maintain the lie, as well. Or maybe she will kill him."

"She hasn't even seen it yet, and she has theories," her husband said, shaking his head and nudging my father with his elbow. The two men laughed at Margaret's expense, but she was too excited to be concerned with their teasing.

"All of the reviews raved about the surprise ending, but I'm not so sure I'll be surprised," she said.

"Your theory sounds plausible to me," I admitted. Especially since I knew nothing at all about the play. Despite Phineas St. Clair's appeal, he seemed to draw a decidedly older audience than one would expect. My friends knew of him but no one had mentioned the play to me.

"Alice," my mother said, grabbing my arm and pulling me back. I startled and then righted myself just in time to have my fingers gripped by a newcomer I did not recognize. "Meet Percy Hughes."

"Percival," the young man before me corrected gently, lowering his head in greeting. "No one has called me Percy since I was a boy. Lovely to see you, Alice. I've heard nothing but good things."

I wondered if he was only being polite and claiming to have heard anything about me, but I was distracted from my thoughts by his ascending the last few stairs into the hall proper. Several steps down, he'd been at my eye level. Now, I had to crane my head back to see him properly.

Percival towered over the crowd. Heaven help the person whose seat was behind his in the theatre. He stood head and shoulders above my father, who I had always deemed a formidable man.

"Percy's father is a friend of your Papa," my mother

reminded. "You two probably have not seen one another since you were little."

"I can't imagine Percival ever being little," I said truthfully.

My mother and Percy both laughed as though it was the funniest thing they'd ever heard, and in their hysterics, I looked to my left and saw a woman I recognized as Percy's mother. She was standing close to his equally tall father. I remembered them both, though Percival still didn't ring any bells. They stood together, whispering and glancing in the direction of our meeting, which had clearly been arranged.

My mother lowered her head and nodded to the young man, encouraging me to speak with him.

Despite my many assurances that I was not in search of a suitor at the present moment, my mother could not pass up the opportunity to arrange a meeting for me. With Catherine now married and a mother, my own mother assumed I must want what she had. Which could not be further from the truth.

I loved Catherine and her husband Charles dearly, and I would love my nieces and nephews just as equally, but as of now, I did not want that settled kind of life. I wanted the kind of adventure Rose and Achilles shared, racing off to Los Angeles to pursue a case, tracking down criminals all over the world. I did not wish to be the woman who endured a lifetime of neck troubles from looking up at the likes of Percival Hughes.

Being rude was not the aim, so I politely engaged Percival for several minutes before excusing myself to speak with a non-existent friend in the crowd. I saw my mother comfort the young man for a moment, probably attempting to excuse my dismissive behavior, before finding another one of her friends with an unmarried son.

I suddenly wished we had been late to the theatre. At least then we would have been forced to rush inside and take our seats, or possibly not attend at all if my father had any say in the matter. Both options would have been better than being subjected to my mother's attempts at matchmaking.

I talked to and subtly let down two more handsome, yet bland suitors before the doors to the theatre opened, and we were allowed to go in and take our seats.

If the lobby seemed grand, the theatre itself was on another plane of existence entirely.

The walls were innately carved and detailed in the same gold as the dome in the lobby. Red velvet curtains hung from the private boxes and draped across the stage like the skirts of an elegant lady's dress. The seats were the same shade of red, and as uncomfortable as I knew they would be, they looked beautiful in the space.

Since our tickets had been gifts from the owner of The Royal Coliseum, we sat in his private box just to the right of the second-floor balcony. It allowed an unobstructed view of the stage and gave us a bird's eye view of the orchestra.

My father handed me a pair of opera glasses, and I lifted them to my eyes, adjusting to the magnification. In the box directly across from us, I could see a young girl tugging at the collar of what looked to be a very itchy dress. The lights had not even gone down yet, and she was already being chastised by her mother to sit still. I wanted to tell her that she would one day enjoy the expe-

rience, though that would have been little comfort
to her.

"You came."

I turned just as Mr. Williamson stepped into our box,
his arms open in greeting. He shook my father's hand and
then kissed both mine and my mother's knuckles.

"I'm so glad you accepted my offer," he said. "Usually,
I stop by the ticket counter to see if the tickets I reserve
have been claimed, but we have been so busy preparing
for the show tonight that I didn't get the chance. I
happened to be walking by the stairs and thought I'd
come see if you were here."

"We are," my father said. "Eleanor could not resist the
offer of a night at the theatre."

"I planned to come and see the play, anyway, but now
we get to see it from the best seat in the house."

Mr. Williamson puffed his chest out slightly. "It is a
rather remarkable view. I should sell the tickets, but I
can't resist keeping them for myself and my dearest
friends. Besides, the favor is always returned to me in one
way or another."

My father did not miss this very obvious hint—as few
people could have—and he quickly invited Mr.
Williamson shooting at our family estate in the country.

"It will be a few weeks yet before we go out to Somerset, but you should join our party. Without you, the
conversation will be all facts and figures. We could use a
bit of variation."

"See what I mean?" Mr. Williamson asked, raising his
brows at my mother. "My generosity never goes unre-
warded. Really, for an offer like that, I should give you the
box seat for every performance we host. I would be

delighted to join your party. It has been far too long since I've killed something. And a man ought to kill something every now and again."

"That's my motto," my father claimed, though I'd never heard him say such a thing. Who would? I knew plenty of men who had never killed a thing, animal or otherwise, though I forced myself not to think of Edward. Still, I smiled and did not deny Mr. Williamson what he clearly believed to be a very witty comment.

"Anyway," he said, shaking my father's hand again. "I really need to be going. Since it is the first night, there will be a thousand problems to work through. Backstage might already be on fire by now."

"Oh, I'm sure it will go perfectly. It sounds so exciting," Mama said.

"You should come see for yourself," Mr. Williamson said. "We are hosting a tour tomorrow morning. You all three should come and see how things operate backstage."

My mother sat up in her seat, excited, before sinking down into her chair, a frown furrowing her brow. "Oh no, we can't. We have a prior engagement."

"Yes, we do," my father said, sounding surprisingly disappointed.

"What of you, Miss Alice?" Mr. Williamson asked, straightening his bow tie and jacket. "You are welcome to come alone if you'd like. You might even get to meet Phineas St. Clair."

"What a wonderful offer. She'd love to," my mother said before I could even open my mouth. "That is too kind."

Mr. Williamson accepted my mother's word as my

own and gave one final nod of his head before leaving to take care of his theatre.

"That will be so fun for you," my mother whispered as the lights dimmed. "Meeting Phineas St. Clair. What a story to tell your friends."

Part of me thought my mother might have accepted the offer because of her own desire to meet the young actor, though I didn't say so. As much as I disliked that she'd accepted on my behalf, it did seem like an interesting way to spend a Saturday morning. It would be more entertaining than reading Rose's letter for the thirteenth time, anyway.

There was no time to discuss the subject further, as the curtain was now rising.

Unfortunately, the description of the show proved to be much more entertaining than the performance itself. As time wore on, the only really positive aspects that caught my interest were the glittering set pieces and the dramatic lighting. During strategic moments, the electrical lights were dimmed to allow the spectacle to be enhanced by a natural glow of candlelight coming from a ring of candles circling the stage. But when the glare of the electrical lights returned in the next scene, the enchantment of the candlelight was lost.

I spent the first hour of the three-hour-long show trying to decide whether it was the writing or the acting that brought down my enjoyment. After an especially emotional scene between Phineas St. Clair and his co-star, Rosalie Stuart, I deemed it to be the writing. The cast delivered their lines with depth of emotion and sincerity, but the words all fell flat.

"*Richard,*" Rosalie's character said to Phineas, the

trembling of her lower lip visible to everyone in the theatre. *"I know much in our lives is false, but my love for you is real."*

"And my love for you is like our bank account," Phineas said, turning away from his on-stage wife and marching across the stage. *"Dwindling more and more every day."*

At this point in the play, the couple had gone from poverty to riches with nothing more than their good looks and charm. However, their lies had grown increasingly desperate and more and more people were becoming suspicious. I suspected it wouldn't be long before the murder discussed in the play's description would happen.

Rosalie burst into tears, her hands covering her face. *"How could you say such a thing, Richard? Don't you love me anymore?"*

I sighed and lifted the opera glasses to my eyes, glancing around at the audience to see if I was the only person desperate for intermission. Perhaps, my love of theatre had not grown with age. Perhaps, I still disliked it just as much as I had in my youth.

I looked across the theatre at the balcony opposite ours and saw the little girl in the itchy dress nodding off in her seat. Her mother elbowed her in the arm when she drifted off of her armrest and onto her mother's, but after a slight adjustment in her seat, she went right back to sleep. I wished I could do the same without judgment. No one would find it as endearing when a woman nearing nineteen dozed off in her seat.

The rest of the audience seemed neutral at best, not exactly the reaction one wanted during an emotional high point in the play. I turned my glasses back towards the stage, scanning over the sides of the stage and the rafters above, trying to see the intricately moving parts of the backstage experience as Mr. Williamson had described them. Then, I lowered the glasses just in time to see Phineas St. Clair throw up his arms in anger and flee from the advances of his on-stage wife. She had tried to cling to him, begging him to love her, but he would not be swayed.

"If our lies have taught me anything, it is that you can only lie for so long. Even to yourself." He dragged a hand through his wavy blonde hair and gazed out at the audience thoughtfully. *"I don't believe I ever really loved you. Not the way I should have. We had fun together, lying and cheating our way to the top, but now it might be time for us to part ways."*

Rosalie's character, whose name I could not remember, jumped to her feet and wiped her tears. *"You forget that I know your lies better than anyone. I know when you are telling one, and you are telling one now. You love me. You have always loved me, but now you are afraid we are going to lose everything, and you think you'll float to the surface of it all if you cut me loose. Well, I won't let that happen."*

"You don't get a say in everything, Victoria."

Victoria. That was her name. I logged the name in my brain, hoping I could finally remember it. Mother and her friends would not look on me kindly if I left this highly anticipated play without remembering the names of the two main characters. Richard and Victoria.

"I will do as I please," Richard continued. *"And there is nothing you can do to stop me."*

Victoria rose to her feet, hands fisted at her sides. *"You don't know what I'm capable of. Leave me, and you won't live to regret it."*

"Are you threatening me?" Richard asked with a cold laugh.

Despite my earlier feelings on the show and my continued belief that it was poorly written, I found myself nearing the edge of my seat. The tension had risen, and I wondered whether Madge's prediction wouldn't be proven right. Maybe one of the main characters would kill the other.

Victoria opened her mouth, probably to inform her stage husband that it was not a threat, but a promise. However, before she could get the words out of her mouth, there was a loud cracking sound.

Everyone, including the actors on stage, jolted at the noise. Before anyone could determine what the sound was or from what direction it had come, a large piece of equipment came falling from the ceiling and crashed onto the stage below.

I was shocked with the rest of the audience that some-thing like that could happen. Clearly, this could not be part of the show. Richard and Victoria were in their luxu-rious home in this scene, so they would not have had a wooden rod with a large metal light affixed to it as ceiling décor. Even if they had, there would have been no reason for it to fall down. This had to be one of the many disas-ters Mr. Williamson had referenced, but unfortunately, this problem did not get solved before the performance.

I was about to turn to my mother and remark on what the actors would do now that they had to work around a large piece of stage equipment in the middle of their set. It might be better to just pull the curtain and start the scene over. All of the tension had been lost, anyway, stolen by the falling debris.

Then, began the screaming.

First, it came from Rosalie Stuart and the patrons seated near the orchestra. Slowly, screams gave way to exclamations of horror and shock, and I looked closer.

At the same moment the people backstage pulled the red velvet curtains closed, I realized that the large piece of equipment had not merely fallen onto the stage. It had fallen directly on Phineas St. Clair.

3

There was no announcement made or directions given for what the audience was to do after the curtains closed. Men and women in the first several rows—who had seen the brunt of the impact—were crying out and fighting to get up and leave, but the rest of the audience sat in a stunned kind of waiting. After several minutes had passed with no word and much of the audience on the ground level was gone, my parents decided we should leave, as well.

"I hope he's all right," my mother said, her eyes wide and stunned. "I didn't really see it happen."

"Something that heavy falling from that height..." My father paused and shook his head.

The outcome couldn't be good. Even without knowing what had happened, I knew that. Phineas St. Clair was hurt, surely.

It wasn't until we reached the lobby that we began to understand the full extent of the situation.

"Blood," a woman sobbed, pressing her husband's

handkerchief to her mouth. "I've never seen so much blood."

I turned to my mother at the same time she looked at me, both of our expressions saying the same thing. *Did you see the blood?*

I shook my head. We had a good view of the stage, but in the dim lighting required of the scene, the stage floor had been mostly in darkness.

"He wasn't even visible under the equipment," a man said quietly. "I don't see how anyone could have survived it."

I heard someone else say, "Do you think they will offer to return everyone's money for the tickets? Surely, they won't continue the play now that the main actor is dead. He has an understudy, but this feels like an omen. If I was any of the other cast members, I'd get out of this theatre immediately."

Part of me thought everyone was overreacting. People tended to jump to the worst possible conclusions, especially when faced with an unexpected crisis like this one. It was irresponsible of the theatre, really, to not come out immediately and comfort the audience. Mr. Williamson should have assured everyone that Phineas was receiving proper medical care. I did see several doctors rush through the curtains in the aftermath, after all. The rumors would be circulating like wild now. He would probably have to issue a public statement in the paper.

Those doubts were still circling in my mind when we stepped through the front doors of the theatre and looked down the high steps to the coroner's vehicle parked along the curb.

My mother gasped, a hand clamped over her mouth. "Oh my. Do you think he really is dead?"

"They don't call the coroner for the living," a passing man said gruffly.

My father narrowed his eyes at the man's back and wrapped an arm around my mother's shoulders. "I don't think he could have survived an accident like that, Eleanor. The light fell from a great height and directly onto his head."

My mother sunk into my father's side while I stood next to them, stunned.

I'd seen dead bodies. More than my fair share, perhaps. Yet, I had never grown accustomed to the sight.

"Stage lights don't just fall like that."

I turned to see a middle-aged gentleman with a thick mustache and balding head punch his hat back into shape before putting it on. He lifted his chin, lips pressed together in suspicion.

"You heard the cracking sound," his equally balding companion said. "We all did. It simply snapped off. Materials can wear over time. If they weren't properly maintained, then it is possible they could—"

"Break off at the exact moment a famous actor is standing beneath?" the mustachioed man finished. "Coincidences like that don't exist."

"You think he was murdered?" his friend asked.

"Why not? Famous people are always being killed for one reason or another. Money, most likely. Or an affair. I've read Phineas St. Clair's name enough times in the paper to know he has a reputation. It wouldn't be so unusual if it caught up with him."

His friend snorted. "You think one of his jilted lovers

lifted her skirts to climb into the rafters and seek revenge? Wouldn't it be easier to just poison him?"

"Of course, it would be easier. But not wiser. Poison says murder. A light falling from the ceiling says tragic accident. A clever woman would know the death of a famous actor would need to be an accident."

The two men walked down the steps together, and I resisted the urge to follow them.

Was it possible they were right and this hadn't been an accident? The thought hadn't even crossed my mind before. Shock, most likely, kept me from thinking of anything but the moment of the accident itself. The confusion of being ripped suddenly and violently out of a fictional scene and into a real-life horror had kept me from asking too many questions. Now, however, I couldn't shake the possibility from my mind.

Moments before the accident, I'd been scanning the crowd and the scene. I replayed the images to the best of my memory in hopes of remembering something, anything that could have explained the tragedy that occurred next.

I'd been trying to get a glimpse of the active backstage life Mr. Williamson had mentioned, but had I noticed a darker side to that world?

I could remember seeing a man in all black crouching in the rafters, but by the looks of him, he'd been focusing his spotlight firmly on the actress sharing the scene with Phineas. Besides, his light had not been the one that had fallen. No one else had been visible to me, but surely if someone had been up there tampering with equipment, the other people operating lights would have noticed, wouldn't they?

"We should leave before this scene becomes even more chaotic," my father said, laying a hand on my mother's lower back. "George won't be here for several more hours, so I'll find us a cab if they aren't already all claimed."

My mother went easily with my father, but I had more questions. I couldn't leave now. Not yet.

I quickly slipped off my long white glove and shoved it into my clutch. "Oh no."

My mother and father both turned to make sure I was all right. I held up my bare hand. "My glove."

Mama frowned, probably wondering how I could have made it all the way outside with only one glove on.

"I left it inside."

"We'll buy you new gloves, Alice," my father said. "Come along. It's madness in there."

"It must be in the box," I said, already turning back for the doors. "I'll go and find it. It will only take a moment."

"Alice," my father called, trying to stop me. I ignored him and raced back across the landing and through the doors of the theatre.

The lobby had filled even more now, the rest of the audience making their way from their seats towards the doors. Staff members dealt with disgruntled customers as best they could, but it was clear they didn't have any answers. Mr. Williamson was no doubt dealing with police and the coroner. The last thing on his mind would be returning the cost of everyone's ticket purchases.

"Come back tomorrow," a young employee said. "We will have answers for you tomorrow. It will be arranged for you to see another showing or receive your money back, but I cannot offer that to you at this moment."

The small crowd around him roared in protest, and the man stumbled back, overwhelmed. I felt for him, but his distraction allowed me to bypass him without notice and move through the door marked "employees" directly behind him.

Unlike the audience entrance which was wide and tall, offering a grand reveal of the full theatre, the employee entrance was short and narrow. The walls seemed to close in on me as I walked down a narrow hallway that ran the length of the theatre. Doors dotted the right side of the hallway, leading into closets and offices, but no one was in there right now. Everyone was probably backstage, which was where I intended to be, as well.

The hallway ended in a sharp left turn and a set of five stairs that led to a door. I mounted them and opened it, and immediately found myself in the wings of the stage.

The curtains, bright red on the outside, were lined in black on the stage-side, casting the entire area in deep inky shadows. Ropes and pipes and pulleys zig-zagged in every direction so my eyes didn't know which way to look.

I could see the backdrop that had last been used in the play—a lavish interior wall complete with gold painted details and wooden trim—but behind it were several more layers of set designs, ready to be slid and positioned when necessary. Except, there was no one there to maneuver them.

Everyone backstage had left their posts, moving instead to the center of the now-shuttered stage. A large group of twenty or more people stood around where I knew Phineas St. Clair must be. People were weeping, and as they were backstage hands, they were already dressed all in black as though knowing they'd be mourning one of their own that night. No one could have known this would happen, though.

Could they?

I took slow, casual steps to the very edge of the stage until I was able to see the sheet-covered lump in the middle of the floor that must have been the actor. Blood dotted the white sheet and spilled across the floor, and if there had been any doubt of his demise, it was gone now.

Rosalie Stuart stood near the backdrop, crying into the arms of an older woman with curly black and gray hair that was twisted into a bun on the back of her neck.

It felt unfair to assess Rosalie based on such an unconventional moment, but she looked much different up close than she had from the stage. Her face was caked in pale powder that made the dabs of blush on her cheeks look clownish. And her eyes were painted with thick liner that was now cascading down her cheeks.

I wondered whether Phineas St. Clair didn't look similarly silly under the sheet, and then chastised myself for the thought. The man was dead. It did not matter what his stage makeup looked like. Especially considering there might not be much of it left if my father was right about the weight of the debris and the height of the fall.

The gruesome image flashed across my mind, and I blinked it away, trying to focus on the scene in front of me.

Everyone, both actors and stage hands, was distressed

and weeping, watching as the coroner moved through his examination. I used their distraction as an opportunity to step forward and look up at the rafters.

It was obvious where the light had fallen from. Directly in the center of a long rafter dotted at regular intervals with large metal lights, there was one missing. Like a jewel fallen from a necklace, the gap was obvious.

It was hard at this distance—and with the glare of the other lights obscuring my vision and casting the gap into darkness—to see how the light would have been affixed to the rafter, but it looked as though there were secondary supports in place to stop an accident like this from happening. Wooden braces moved from the back of the lights to a second rafter running along the length of the main one, and my best guess was that the wood snapping loose had been the crack the audience had heard just prior to the light falling.

I followed the trajectory of the light down from the rafters to the ground where Phineas still lay, and then looked directly back from that spot and saw the piece of splintered wood lying on the stage. I needed to look at it in order to see if it had cracked of natural causes or due to being tampered with.

I took a step forward, prepared to test my luck and walk onto the stage proper when suddenly, two figures shifted back from the group, stopping me in my tracks.

It was a man and a woman. I did not recognize either of them, but they both appeared to be in ordinary clothes. Nothing identified them as either actors or stage hands, though they certainly weren't dressed as an audience member as I was.

The man, tall and thin with mousy brown hair,

leaned down to speak to the woman at an intimate distance. The woman seemed drawn to him, her body leaning closer to his as though she couldn't help herself. She nodded at whatever he said to her and then looked back at the scene before her, shaking her head sadly.

In comparison to the man, who struck me as rather plain, the woman was vibrant. She had curly red hair, pale skin, and bright red lips. She was also full-figured, which was obvious despite the boxy shape of the dress she wore.

I stared at them and then down at the wood located only a few steps behind them. There was no way I could grab it without their noticing, and I couldn't stay backstage for much longer before my parents would come looking for me.

I bit my lip, trying to decide what to do, but before I could come to any kind of conclusion, the man leaned down to whisper something else and then, to my utter disbelief, he smiled.

The expression stopped my thoughts cold.

True, people responded differently to tragedy. Some people liked to carry on as though nothing had changed, others liked to mourn and weep for days, and still others, like myself, wanted to find solutions. However, I had never seen someone smile like that in the presence of a corpse before. That kind of expression simply made no sense, and I frowned, wishing I could hear what it was he was saying to the woman.

While I was still trying to read his lips, the man's mouth stopped moving, and I glanced up to his eyes, realizing with horror that he was staring directly at me. His smile had faded, replaced by a furrowed brow and an expression of confusion.

I looked away quickly, wondering whether I should make a quick escape or try to seem as though I belonged. That would be difficult given my formal gown, but perhaps if I appeared confident, the man would say nothing. He didn't look like a person who would carry much weight with the rest of the cast and crew anyway. Maybe, like me, he was a curious onlooker who had wandered in from the streets.

"Are we actors not entitled to private death and grieving like the rest of the world?" the man said suddenly and loudly.

My eyes shot back to him, as did everyone else's in the room. He was an actor. I had not seen him on stage, but he had just identified himself as one. I wanted to melt into the cracks of the stage.

"Why is there an audience member back here?" he asked. "The stage should be closed."

The previously distracted crowd all turned their eyes on me, and I felt like all of the spotlights had been aimed at me. Heat rolled down my back, and I took a step away, hoping I'd be able to slip back into the shadows.

"I'm sorry," I whispered, as though I had interrupted a performance rather than an impromptu wake. "I was just lost. I didn't mean to—"

The man waved his arm in a sweeping motion, gesturing for someone to escort me away, and when no one volunteered for the job, the red-haired woman next to him jumped into action. She crossed the stage with several loud clicks of her heels across the wood floor, grabbed my arm, and hauled me through the door, down the stairs, and into the narrow employee hallway.

The path wasn't wide enough for us to walk shoulder to shoulder, so the women let go of my arm and walked behind me, staying close behind even as I tried to increase my pace to get away from her.

"I'm sorry," I said again. "I wasn't trying to be disrespectful. I didn't even know Phineas St. Clair. Not the way a lot of other people seemed to. I simply came back to look for a lost glove, and—"

"Don't let anyone else hear you say that," she said, cutting me off and sounding surprisingly amused.

"What?"

"That you didn't care about Phineas," she said. "It is better if they at least think you were a great admirer of his acting. If you just came backstage to see a dead body, it looks much worse for you."

"That wasn't why I was there," I argued. "I just wanted to—"

"I don't care either way," she said. "I worked with Phineas but was not particularly close with him. Not the way other members of the cast were."

The woman was being kinder than I thought she would be based on the rough way she'd grabbed my arm on stage, so I slow my pace slightly. "Like the man you were standing next to?"

"Alfred Grey. And yes, he was the understudy for the Richard character. He and Phineas ran lines before every show." She sighed. "That is why he was so upset you were back there. Of course, it is a section of the theatre that is for stage workers only, so you shouldn't have been there, but he wouldn't have usually been so blunt. He is a very nice man."

"He seemed it," I said quietly, barely hiding my sarcasm.

"I know you," the woman said.

My next step stuttered, and I looked back over my shoulder. "Excuse me?"

"I've heard of you, anyway."

The newspapers. Edward's crime. I always seemed to forget that my face was now recognizable. "Well, my brother's sins have nothing to do with me, so—"

"Oh, no," she said. "I mean, I do know your picture from the news stories, but I also know who you are because my cousin works in your family's home."

I came to a full stop and turned around. "Who?"

"Louise. She has red hair like mine, though that is as far as our similarities go. She just started as—"

"A maid," I finished, nodding. "Yes, I know her. She is a little flighty, but a nice girl."

"That is like Louise," she said, smiling fondly. Then, she held out her hand. "Judith. I do the costumes for the tour company. Well, I did. I suppose I should go see if I still have a job."

I wanted to offer some kind of comforting word or ask her more questions, but it seemed like a poor time, and I didn't know how to phrase the words in a way that wouldn't seem disrespectful. So, I simply waved and then walked into the lobby, blending in with the few remaining audience members making their way through the doors and outside.

4

"I can't believe they don't have more about it in the paper," my mother said, turning the front page of the paper back and forth, as if hoping for more words to appear.

"There will be a bigger write-up tomorrow, you can count on it," my father assured her. "It only happened last night."

"If the death of a celebrated actor at a famous London theatre is not the kind of news that would force you to stay up all night rearranging the paper, then I don't understand journalism at all."

My father glanced up at her, his mouth quirking up in a sly smile, silently mocking the fact that she had hardly read a newspaper before this morning, so she really didn't know anything about journalism. Wisely, he kept those jokes to himself.

"It's offensive," she said, throwing the paper to the side. "He was a well-respected man in his field. He deserves more than a paragraph. Especially after dying the way he died." She pressed a hand to her chest and closed her eyes. "It was horrible."

"Then don't think about it anymore," my father offered, lifting his own paper up like a wall.

My mother rolled her eyes at him and looked at me, her face pulled down with concern. "How are you doing this morning, Alice? Are you faring all right? I wish we'd never taken you to the theatre with us."

"I'm fine," I assured her. "We were too far away to see anything too horrible. It was sad, but I am not devastated."

"Not like Madge." Mama pointed to the note that had arrived first thing that morning. "She and her husband were sitting ten rows back, and she saw the entire thing. Having those images in her head was not enough, though. She had to write about them in excruciating detail in the letter. I might never forgive her."

"Madge was so excited to see Phineas in person," I said sadly, hoping to stir some sympathy in my mother's heart for her friend, even though I knew she'd forgive Margaret as soon as they saw one another next. She couldn't stay angry with her for long.

"We all were. Mr. Williamson said something about introducing us last weekend, but that won't happen now."

"Yes, that is the tragedy here," my father said dryly.

Mama frowned at the back of his newspaper and then violently stuck her fork into her eggs. "Of course, his death is the tragedy. It was a horrible accident. Terrible. Unthinkable. I hope Mr. Williamson won't face any charges over it." She gasped, like the idea had surprised her. "Do you think Mr. Williamson could be in any trouble, James?"

He lowered his paper, mouth twisted to one side in thought, and then shrugged. "It's possible. He could be held liable for the death. Especially if they determine it was faulty equipment or poor maintenance."

"Hopefully not," my mother said. "It was not his fault."

"It might not be," I said, remembering the theory the two men outside the theatre had posed. "Maybe someone did it on purpose."

My mother's attention snapped to me, her mouth hanging open in shock. "Alice. You can't be serious."

"It is just a possibility," I said meekly. I thought the idea might ease her worries about Mr. Williamson, but murder was clearly not a happy thought regardless of the alternative.

"Actors are known to be quite dramatic," Papa said. "Who knows what could have been transpiring behind the scenes. We could have witnessed a murder."

"James," Mama chastised. "Do not joke about such things, and do not encourage Alice's wild ideas. It was an accident. Nothing like that could have been planned."

I wanted to disagree with her, but I held my tongue. If my mother had any inkling at all I wanted to further investigate the case, she would never let me out of her sight.

As it was, I stayed quiet about my suspicions, and, after breakfast, my mother returned to her room to lie down before she and my father left for the day. That was when I casually found my way to the kitchen.

Much like my parents had been that morning, the kitchen staff was huddled around a discarded newspaper, listening as one of the cooks read the article aloud.

"Mr. St. Clair was attended to by several doctors from the audience, but they determined nothing could be done for him. Funeral arrangements will be announced in the days ahead."

"Is that it?"

"There has to be more," they said, talking over one another. "What happened? I heard he was crushed."

"But by what?"

"A light from the ceiling," I said.

All at once, the group of four jumped, dropping the paper, and looked guiltily up at me.

I held up my hands. "I'm sorry. I didn't mean to frighten anyone."

"Sorry, Miss," Francine said, lowering her head. She was my mother's age and made my favorite croissant in all of the world. "Curiosity got the better of us, I suppose. Come on now, girls. Get back to work."

"It's fine," I assured them all, even as they dispersed and began cleaning up the dishes left over from breakfast. "I didn't come in here to make sure you were working. I came to talk."

The younger kitchen staff looked up at me with obvious curiosity. Mary, a bird-like blonde with big green eyes frowned. "Begging your pardon, Miss, but you were at the theatre with your parents when it happened, weren't you?"

Francine hissed at the girl, but I nodded. "Yes, I was. A light broke free of the rigging above the stage and crushed Phineas where he stood. It was horrible."

Even Francine couldn't contain herself. She dropped the pan she'd been scrubbing into the soapy water and turned back to me. "Did he die instantly? Did he suffer?"

"I think it was fast, but I can't be sure. We were in a second-floor balcony. We didn't have much of a view."

"Thank Heaven for that," she said, pressing her thumb against her lips, even the imagined memory too much for her to bear.

"I didn't really know much about Phineas St. Clair before yesterday," I admitted. "I came to see if any of you were more familiar with his work than I am."

They all look at one another before turning back to me.

"I haven't been to any of his shows if that is what you mean, Miss," Francine said.

"Did you ever read about him in the paper?"

Francine tipped her head back and narrowed her eyes. "Gossip, you mean?"

My mouth turned up in a smile, and I nodded sheepishly. "Yes, I suppose that is what I mean."

Francine hitched a thumb over her shoulder at the younger girls standing behind her. "Then you came to the right place."

The girls were eager to help, though they didn't offer me much information that I didn't already know.

Phineas St. Clair was very popular with the female population. He was rumored to be with a different woman in every city he stopped at, though none seriously. He had never been engaged or even connected to the same woman for very long. He seemed to enjoy the touring lifestyle, and he used it to his advantage.

Most of the information the girls had revolved around his wealth. Different numbers were thrown out from staggeringly low to staggeringly high, but there was no consensus on whether Phineas St. Clair was actually worth anything or not.

"That is why he was constantly touring," one of the cooks said. "Because he had no money. He was desperate."

"He was born into a wealthy family, which means he did not have to work. He was doing it for the pure passion," another girl argued.

Despite none of them having seen him perform, they argued the merits of his talent. I was just about to thank them and excuse myself when the door behind me opened and Louise walked in.

Her head was tipped to the side, her arms wrapped around a basket of dirty linens from one of the bedrooms upstairs, and she had a vacant smile on her face. She was halfway into the kitchen before she seemed to notice anyone was in there at all, and she'd greeted the rest of the staff before she noticed me. When she did, her spine straightened, and her eyes widened.

"Miss Beckingham," she said, tipping her head in greeting.

"Louise," I nodded and smiled.

"Good you are here, Louise," one of the cooks said. "Miss Beckingham came to ask us about Phineas St. Clair."

Louise's smile faltered. "Horrible news. Poor man."

The other girl nodded impatiently. "Yes, yes, terrible, but your cousin works for the company, doesn't she?"

Louise frowned as if she wasn't sure, and then smiled. "She does. A costumer."

"Judith. Yes, I met her yesterday," I said.

"You did?" Everyone in the room looked confused at that revelation, but I just nodded.

"I met her after the accident. I...ran into her backstage. She recognized me as the daughter of your employer and introduced herself." There was a high probability Judith would explain the full circumstances about our meeting to Louise at a later date, but I would let her do that. I decided my pared down version was as truthful as I needed to be.

I was just about to ask Louise if Judith had mentioned anything about what it was like to work closely with Phineas St. Clair, but before I could, the door opened again. This time, the staff jolted in surprise and got to work immediately, scattering like startled pigeons.

"Louise," my mother said from behind me. She came to stand next to me and then seemed surprised to see me in the kitchen. However, she quickly refocused as Louise moved to stand in front of her.

"Lady Ashton," she said, hands folded behind her back.

"Louise, dear," my mother said gently, though I recognized the annoyance in her voice. It was a tone she had reserved for me for the majority of my life. "I asked you to do the ironing today."

"It is done," Louise said, bobbing her head once in emphasis.

"Yes, I saw that," Mama said. "The problem, dear, is that you ironed the laundry and then re-folded it."

A groan came from the direction of Francine, but she disguised it with a cough.

Louise blinked up at my mother in obvious confusion.

"They need to be re-ironed and hung up," my mother explained. "When you folded them, you put creases back in the clothes."

"Oh." Louise winced. "I'm sorry, Lady Ashton. I'll go and do it properly right now."

Louise hurried out of the kitchen, and my mother laid one hand on her forehead and the other on my shoulder. "Louise is sweet." It sounded more like a reminder to herself than anything else.

Somewhere in the distance, a church bell rang announcing it was ten o'clock in the morning, and my mother jumped as though she'd been the one struck with a mallet. "Oh, Alice. The theatre."

"Yes?"

"The tour," she explained. "Backstage. Mr. Williamson. It starts soon."

"Surely they aren't still doing that. A man died."

"No one has called to announce it was cancelled," she said, wrapping an arm around my waist and pulling me towards the door. "So, you should hurry and make sure you don't miss it. You don't want to be rude."

"I'm sure Mr. Williamson wouldn't even notice. He is going to be so busy managing all the chaos from the accident. He won't care a thing about a silly tour."

"I care," she said. "Mr. Williamson and his theatre need our support more than ever. It will be a good show of faith that you still went to the theatre after the accident."

I tried to argue, but she was already pushing me towards the stairs. Besides, it would give me a good excuse to get backstage again and do some more investigating. So, I followed her prodding.

"Wear something nice and smile for the onlookers," she said. "You want to look happy to be there. For Mr. Williamson!"

I resisted sighing and nodded, practicing my fake smile as I disappeared into my room and changed into more suitable attire.

5

Not only was the theatre still doing the behind the scenes tour, but there were more people there than I ever could have imagined. Based on the way the theatre staff were frantically running around, I assumed a lot of the people simply showed up after hearing the news of Phineas St. Clair's death in hopes of hearing the latest details.

I pushed my way through the doors and into the lobby where a large group of people were gathered. Two employees were standing in front of the group with their arms stretched out to either side, acting like human barriers, and looking around for some kind of help.

"At this rate, they'll cancel the entire tour," a middle-aged woman complained to her husband. "They should have offered tickets to this. It is chaos now."

"We'll get inside," her husband assured her, though I was on her side. If I was in charge, I would have pushed everyone back outside and locked the doors.

Especially since the police were still moving around

the scene. Policemen came and went through the 'employees only' door I'd walked through the night before, carrying bags of evidence. Everything was surely cleaned up by this point—it wasn't sanitary or humane to leave the actor's dead body in the theatre through the night and into the next day—but there was still probably a lot of evidence to gather and interviews to take.

The heat from the crowd was stifling, and I slipped out of my coat and draped it across my arm. My mother had barely approved of the tan skirt and matching coat with buttons down the front, so I knew she would have been beside herself to see me in just the skirt and a white cotton blouse, but the lobby was too warm for layers. I stretched onto my tip-toes in hopes of seeing an employee or someone in the coat check above the crowd, but the post was unmanned. The well-oiled machine of the theatre I'd seen last night was long gone.

This fact was only punctuated when Mr. Williamson himself stumbled out of a door on the right-hand side of the lobby moving at a near-run. He headed straight towards our group and then bypassed us entirely, running through the doors and outside.

Curious and tired of standing with the other people impatiently waiting to find out when and if the tour would be happening at all, I pushed my way back through the crowd and followed Mr. Williamson's trajectory outside.

I scanned the steps and found him directly in the center of them, addressing a small cluster of newspaper reporters waiting on the sidewalk below.

"The sidewalk is public property, but I've alerted the police to your presence, nonetheless," Mr. Williamson shouted. "If any one of you step foot through that door, you will be arrested. The theatre belongs to me, and I will not have you shoving cameras in the faces of my guests. Take whatever photographs you want out here and leave. You won't be getting any more interviews today."

Following half of his advice, the journalists lifted the cameras and began to snap pictures. The flashes popped and smoked, and when they were done, they continued standing in the exact same place they had been before, unconcerned about Mr. Williamson's threats.

I could see his shoulders sag in defeat, and he mounted the steps with considerably less zeal than he had descended them. When he reached the top of the stairs, I had to say his name to keep him from running into me.

"Oh," he said, obviously startled. He rocked on his feet, but balanced himself quickly. When he recognized me, he smiled, though it did not reach his eyes. "Miss Alice. I'm so glad you accepted my offer. Had I known the place would be turned on its head like this, I never would have suggested you come. In fact, you should go home and come another day. A respectable young lady like you does not need to be in this wild atmosphere. Did any journalists trouble you on your way in? If so, I will have them arrested. Point them out to me."

A young reporter in a too-large suit and a mismatched hat had asked me very politely if I'd been at the show the night before and what my business was at the theatre today, but I'd declined to answer any of his questions, and he'd let me pass without incident. Certainly not the kind of behavior that warranted an arrest.

"No one troubled me," I assured Mr. Williamson, laying a hand on his arm. "Are you doing all right? You seem overwhelmed."

He laughed bleakly. "I am. As if the tragedy last night wasn't enough, I now have to contact every performance company scheduled here for the next six months and convince them they won't be crushed to death by falling set designs."

He sighed and held up a hand. "Apologies. That was gruesome. I shouldn't have—"

"No apology necessary. That is what happened," I said with a shrug. "But surely people aren't really afraid an accident like that could happen again."

"Of course, they are," he said sharply. "The one-man show scheduled for next week pulled out late last night and a four-day musical event tried to pull out this morning. I've convinced them to stay so far, but if the vultures down there publish lies in the papers, I could be ruined."

He looked over his shoulder at the reporters, his upper lip pulled back in a scowl, and then shook his head. Mr. Williamson looked fifteen years older than he had the night before. The stress of the last sixteen hours had settled in the lines of his face, and he was a man in desperate need of a holiday.

"What is the truth?" I asked quietly. "Do the police have any idea what happened?"

"An accident, they say." He shrugged his shoulders, his arm slapping against his leg. "That is the answer they are leaning towards now, and I don't think they are even searching for another possibility."

"Do you want them to search for another answer?"

"I want them to search for the truth," he said, his neck

growing red with passion. "The stage lights and mechanics are checked and maintained before every performance. I personally oversaw the inspection the day before the accident. If a light had been close to falling, we would have seen it and corrected the problem."

"So..." I said, trying to lead Mr. Williamson to say what he meant.

"So," he continued, "the light did not fall because of any fault of the theatre. I do not know what happened to it between the time of our inspection and the time of the accident, but I am not at fault. Yet, I will be the one blamed when this is all said and done. Take my word for it. Phineas St. Clair was a beloved actor, and I will be tried and hung in the court of public opinion just so there can be someone to blame."

"If you know the light did not fall due to a maintenance failure, then how do you think it fell?" I asked.

Mr. Williamson pressed his lips together and glanced back again to be sure no reporters had crept from the public sidewalk to the private stairs. Then, he sighed. "I want the police to answer that question. All I know is it is through no fault of my own."

I deflated slightly. It seemed like he was close to suggesting it could have been a murder, but he held back. So, I would hold back for now, too. Until I had more proof.

"I'm sure the police won't pin the blame on you. This theatre has been in your family for years, and I'm sure it will be for years and years to come."

Mr. Williamson smiled sadly at me and nodded. "I hope you are right."

"I am," I said, feigning more confidence than I felt.

"Mr. Williamson."

I turned around and saw a detective standing in the doorway, a clipboard held to his chest. "We need you to unlock a maintenance room for our investigators."

"Coming." Mr. Williamson sighed and grumbled as he pulled a ring of keys from his pocket and began walking back inside. Suddenly, he stopped and turned back to me. "Would you like me to check your coat? Our staff is scattered across the premises, so I can't guarantee anyone will be available to take care of it, but I don't want you to be inconvenienced."

"You are busy," I said, waving away his gesture. "That is kind of you, but I'll check it myself if I have to."

He seemed relieved not to have to add another thing to his plate, smiled, and left. As soon as he had walked away from our conversation, I felt confident he'd forgotten about me altogether. I couldn't blame him. Mr. Williamson had a great deal on his mind.

Perhaps, if I was lucky, I'd find the evidence necessary to ease some of his worries.

BY THE TIME I made it back inside, the tour group had moved to the center of the lobby and a dark-haired woman with chin-length hair and a brown skirt and matching jacket on was addressing them. I hung my coat in the unmanned coat closet and hurried across the room. I positioned myself near the right side closest to the employee entrance. I saw Mr. Williamson's back just as he was leading the detective down the employee hallway I'd been in the night before.

"Sorry for the delay," the woman said. "The tour group is larger than anticipated, so new arrangements had to be made."

"Will there still be a tour?" a woman in the crowd asked.

"Yes," she assured us all. "The tour is still happening."

"Will the play continue?" someone else asked. There was a murmur of similar questions, and the woman nodded slowly, taking a deep breath as she did.

"After a short break this evening, the actors will continue their performances throughout the rest of the week that they've been scheduled to be here with us."

A sigh of relief moved through the room as a man in a brown suit switched places with the woman and raised his hands to draw the crowd's attention. "The show must go on. I am the director of the production, and Phineas St. Clair was the truest showman I've ever seen. He truly believed in this industry and in his art, and I know he would not want us to cancel shows on his account."

"You don't think his opinion would have changed after being killed on stage?" This voice came from remarkably close to me, and I turned and saw a short, balding man peeking his head over the crowd. "Is it even safe for the other actors?"

"The police will soon rule the death a tragic accident, and the stage and equipment is being checked right now by maintenance," the man said. "Everyone is perfectly safe."

The man lowered his head, and I watched as he pulled a small notebook from his pocket and began taking down notes. Based on that and the ink smudges on the ends of his fingers, it looked like one of the reporters had made it past Mr. Williamson's invisible line in the sand.

The large crowd was split into two more manageable groups and then we were sent in opposite directions. One group was sent backstage to look at the set design and talk with the costume department, while my group was sent into the main theatre.

The dark-haired woman from before led our tour, pointing out the architecture of the building and remarking on the history of the site. I tried to pay attention because the information was interesting, but I couldn't help but be impatient. I wanted to get backstage. I should have slipped away with the first group as soon as I realized where they were going, but a man began talking to me just as the groups were splitting, and I couldn't get away without drawing too much attention.

"We should have gone with the other group."

I jumped at the voice in my ear and turned to see the same man who had halted my escape before standing behind me.

He was quite handsome—golden hair, sun-kissed skin, and a friendly smile—but I was too annoyed with him to care much.

"Are you not enjoying this portion of the tour?"

He shook his head. "No, and it doesn't look as though you are, either."

I smiled. "I'd hoped I was hiding it enough that no one would notice."

"Don't worry. I doubt anyone was paying as much attention to you as I was."

My brow lifted in curiosity, and the man's face flushed with embarrassment. "I'm Thomas."

"Alice," I said, taking his hand. "Are you a lover of the theatre?"

He nodded. "I'd like to be an actor one day. I work at a bank with my father right now, so the closest I can get to being behind the curtains is this tour."

"Your father doesn't approve?"

"He thinks it is a passing fancy. Life is about security, and nothing says security like working in a bank. *People will always need money.*" He lowered his voice and frowned, no doubt emulating his father.

"Based on that impression, we could have the same father." I laughed.

A woman in front of us turned to look over her shoulder with a glare, clearly annoyed that we were interrupting the tour. I lifted a hand in apology and ducked my head, trying to hide a nervous smile.

Thomas leaned forward, voice lowered in a whisper. "What about you? Do you love the theatre?"

"Love is a strong word," I admitted. "I've been to the theatre, but I'm actually here because my family knows the owner."

"Mr. Williamson?" Thomas asked, brow furrowed. "You know him?"

"My parents are long-time friends. He invited me on the tour, and I didn't want to be rude."

"How lucky for me, then," Thomas said with a confident smile.

I had not come here to meet a man, but there seemed to be no reason to turn him away on that account alone. So, he stayed close to my side throughout the tour, and I did not complain.

After half an hour, the two separate tour groups

switched and it was our turn for a backstage tour of the theatre. Rather than walk down the narrow hallway that ran next to the theatre, we were able to file through a hidden door built into the side of the stage.

The cavern inside the stage was tall enough for an average person to stand at their full height, though Thomas and several other members of our group had to duck their heads.

Our tour guide directed us to the back of the space where there was a small set of wooden stairs and another door. We filed up the stairs in an orderly manner and ended up on the stage.

"That route allows cast and crew to move from one side of the stage to the other without the audience noticing," the woman said once everyone was gathered together again. "There is another door on the opposite side of the stage for the same purpose. There is also a set of stairs that leads up to the lights so the crew can operate the equipment during the performance."

At the mention of the lights, the entire tour group seemed to shift uncomfortably. Everyone's gazes slowly drifted towards the unmistakable gap in the rigging and then downward to where it had fallen on the stage.

The scene had been cleaned since I'd been on the stage the night before. There was no sheet-covered lump in the middle of the floor or any blood. Though, I did notice a small dent in the wood where a screw or some other sharp piece of metal had dug into the finish.

The tour guide clapped her hands, making several people jump. "Anyway, while sitting in the audience, the theatre may be a quiet retreat, but backstage, there is a whole world buzzing. Costumers are changing wardrobes

and touching up makeup, the set designer is ensuring the
right props and backdrops are being used for the correct
scenes, and a host of crew are keeping the performance
moving at a non-stop clip. It is very exciting."

As the woman led everyone towards the back of the
stage to admire the careful detail of the set design—the
same gold-detailed backdrop that had been up last night
when the accident occurred—I stepped back.

Now that I was backstage again, it would be the
perfect time to break away from the group and do some
more exploring. There was no roster. No sign-up sheet
where my name had been taken down. The tour guide
was not counting heads at stops along the way, so she
would not notice my absence. I could just end my tour
here and slip away.

Just as I was beginning to break away from the group,
Thomas turned to look for me. When his eyes met mine,
he smiled that handsome—suddenly annoying—smile
and walked over to me.

"I'm with you. I thought they would be telling us
something we didn't already know about theatre. This
tour is not informative at all." He crossed his arms over
his chest and sighed. "A lot of these people seem to be
enjoying it, though."

I gritted my teeth and smiled. This was why I should
not have encouraged his friendship. My opportunity to
investigate had arrived, and I couldn't take it unless I
wanted to explain to Thomas that I was only here to
discover whether Phineas St. Clair was murdered.

There was the possibility Thomas wouldn't mind or
that he would find it interesting, but there was also a
possibility he'd think I was mad and inform the tour

guide at once. Being barred from the theatre for life would not help with my investigation.

I was considering the effectiveness of claiming I had a horrible stomach ache and rushing away from the group in search of a ladies room when the tour guide held up both hands, palms out, in a way that suggested she had a big announcement coming and needed us all to stay calm.

"We have quite the treat for you all," she said, her lips pressed together in a firm smile. "Never one to disappoint her fans, the lead actress, Rosalie Stuart, has decided to come out and answer any questions you all may have for her."

The group bristled, shuffling closer to the tour guide and stretching up on their toes to see from which direction the actress would be coming. Thomas, too, turned his attention from me back to the tour.

Then, from stage right, Rosalie entered.

Her face was pale, though not from stage makeup as it had been the night before. She appeared tired with red around her eyes like she'd been crying. Still, a wide smile was painted across her face, and she lifted her hand in a grand wave.

The tour group clapped and cheered, all attention pinned to the woman as though this itself was a performance. As curious as I was to hear what Rosalie had to say, I knew this was my moment to leave. So, while everyone was focused forward, I pulled away from the group and exited stage left.

The tour guide had mentioned another staircase in the wings that led up to the rigging, but it took me several minutes of circling and squinting into the shadows to find it, as it was hidden behind a heavy black curtain.

According to the guide, everything in the wings on both sides of the stage was covered in dark curtains and everyone wore dark clothing so that if an audience member could see beyond the stage, the magic wouldn't be entirely ruined for them. It would simply look like the mouth of a very dark cavern rather than a wooden skeleton outfitted with ropes and pulleys and levers.

I pulled back the curtain and moved up the stairs slowly, wincing as the wood squealed beneath my feet. I could still hear the tour group shouting questions at Miss Stuart, so I knew they were nearby and would overhear me if I made any loud, sudden movements.

The staircase spiraled upwards and ended in a large wooden platform no more than two paces wide. I expected there to be a wooden railing or some kind of safety guard in place, but there was nothing. I was surprised it wasn't a person that fell from the rafters and crushed Phineas St. Clair. That seemed almost more likely than a light.

A thin bridge spanned the distance of the stage. It seemed to be a clear cut path from one side to the other, but as I walked carefully across the bridge, small platforms like little wooden islands began to appear. Some branched off from the main bridge, others were suspended from the back wall or stood on stilts bracketed to the floor. The small platforms were places where a crew member could sit and control the spotlights as the actors moved around the stage below. It didn't seem that the person at each post could see anyone else very well, especially when the lights were turned on, casting everything in silhouette and shadow.

It became apparent immediately that any single person who had been working up there the night of the accident could have been responsible for the light falling onto the stage below. And judging by how easily I was able to access the space, someone who didn't work up there could have just as easily done the deed.

Effectively, my suspect list had not been narrowed at all, though I knew one thing for certain. It was just as possible that the light had been tampered with as it was that the light had fallen due to poor maintenance.

The height made me feel unsteady, and I felt I'd tempted fate enough by crawling around in the rigging. So, I slowly made my way back to the main platform and then down the stairs.

I sighed when my feet hit solid ground.

"Who are you?"

I jolted, falling back onto the stairs. I righted myself quickly and found Rosalie Stuart standing in front of me, her brows furrowed.

I'd been so focused on getting back down to the stage floor that I hadn't thought to check and see if anyone was coming. I also hadn't been listening for the sound of the tour group anymore. Obviously, Rosalie had ended her question and answer session while I was crawling around in the rafters, and I'd been too distracted to notice. Now, I'd been caught.

"What are you doing back here?" she asked, taking one step away from me as though she was nervous.

If I told her I'd come with the tour group, she would

think me an overenthusiastic admirer and send for someone to remove me from the area immediately. So, I said the first thing that came to my mind—the truth. "I came to investigate the cause of the death of Phineas St. Clair."

"That is what the police are for," she said coldly, looking no less suspicious. Then, her head tilted to the side. "Are you one of Phineas' girlfriends? Do you think that gives you a right to wander around the stage and do as you please? Because it does not." She sighed and pinched the bridge of her nose between her thumb and forefinger. "Honestly, I cannot keep having this conversation. I'm sorry you are upset, but you'll soon learn Phineas had more than his fair share of romantic partners. While younger than most, you are one among many. You will receive no special treatment here. Please leave before I ask the police to remove you."

"I'm not a girlfriend," I said quickly. "I am a friend of Mr. Williamson's."

Rosalie pulled her arms tightly around her waist and the crease in her forehead eased. "Mr. Williamson? The owner of the theatre?"

"Yes. He invited me here."

This was all true. Mr. Williamson had invited me to the theatre today—for the tour, of course, but Rosalie Stuart didn't need to know that.

"Oh." She looked up the stairs I had just come down and over towards the stage. "And you are investigating the death? How so?"

Poorly, so far, considering I'd been caught both times by members of the cast. I needed to be more discreet or I was going to be escorted to the curb with the reporters.

"I'm just looking for every possible explanation," I

said vaguely.

Rosalie narrowed her eyes. "I thought it was an accident."

"Yes, of course," I said. "And Mr. Williamson wants that confirmed. That is why I'm here."

The actress lifted her chin, studying me, and then sighed. "That makes sense. I want things to be thorough, too. I wouldn't say this publicly, but the entire cast is terrified this could happen again. I mean, I was only ten steps away from him. It could have been me!"

Perhaps, I should have mentioned that I was looking into the idea of a murder. Maybe that idea would have comforted Rosalie more than the death being an accident. However, the current story had granted me access to backstage, so I didn't want to do anything to jeopardize that.

"Do you think you could point me in the direction of Mr. St. Clair's dressing room?" I asked.

Rosalie, worries evidently assuaged, agreed and walked me through the stage exit and down another hallway to the dressing rooms. She pointed to one on the left.

"That was his room."

I thanked her at once and then moved towards the door. Taped to the center of it was a piece of paper, pinned there by the police. It was just a notice that the room had been part of the investigation and was now able to be used again, but it reminded me of the speed required in this investigation.

As the saying went, the show must go on. And go on it would, with or without Phineas St. Clair. If I wanted to uncover what happened to him, I couldn't delay.

6

The idea of an actor's dressing room had always elicited images of grandeur. Grandeur not unlike the velvet curtains and gold-foiled detail of the main theatre. The reality was much more modest.

A small desk with scattered script pages and bits and pieces of costume sat in the corner. A large armchair with a blanket thrown over the side was directly in front of the door, a small table with a book atop pressed close to its side. Then, there was a low wooden coffee table with a bowl of fruit and a vase of flowers sitting in front of a tufted two-seat couch, which was pressed against the same wall as the door. A large mirror hung above the couch at a worrying angle from the wall.

Was everything in Phineas St. Clair's life at danger of crashing over his head? If the light hadn't done it, certainly the mirror would have.

Steering clear of the probable trajectory of the mirror should the nail it hung from decide to give up, I pressed the door closed behind me and stepped into the room.

It smelled of smoke and dust, and I had the urge to crack open a window, though there were no windows. Two standing lamps in opposite corners of the room cast the space in a dim yellow glow that, rather than alleviate the glumness, seemed to emphasize it.

This was the last place Phineas St. Clair was before he died.

His death was already not the happiest of topics to be sure, but that reality made it seem even worse. After years of travelling the continent and experiencing the best life had to offer, he'd spent his final moments in a dark, dusty room in the back of a theatre.

I pushed my emotions aside and began a short inventory of the room.

Drawers in the desk were hanging open and all of the furniture seemed to be sitting at slightly wrong angles. The police had searched the room and clearly done a poor job of setting it right again.

Aside from stage makeup and breath mints, the desk held nothing of interest. I flipped through the pages of script on top that had been left behind, and the first page was coincidentally the final scene Phineas had performed before his death. It was the argument between his character and Rosalie Stuart's.

I read through the page, stopping at the moment the light had fallen. The stage direction there said *[she desperately embraces him]*, but it had been crossed out. Rewritten in the margins in ink was: *[he pushes her away, and they stare at one another]*. Several more handwritten notes were scribbled around it. *Emotional distance=physical distance. Separation. More powerful.*

Scripts were changed all the time, though that

seemed a rather convenient change considering what had happened seconds after Phineas pushed Rosalie away. Had it simply been a lucky break for Rosalie that she hadn't been crushed, as well, while embracing him? Or had someone planned it that way?

I flipped through the script and saw other similar notes written in the margins, so it was hard to say whether this change was especially unusual or not.

The book next to the chair was thick and leather bound, but when I tried to open it, the spine was still stiff. Phineas' name was written in the front cover, but it was obvious he had scarcely opened it before. He had certainly never read it. And now he never would.

Unless I wanted to dig through cushions and look under furniture, the room held little else to explore. I didn't know if the police had taken most of Phineas' things with them after their investigation or if this was truly all he travelled with. Regardless, there was little else I could do in terms of an investigation.

I sighed and flopped down on the sofa, disappointed. My eyes scanned the coffee table, and that was when I noticed the vase of flowers.

I'd seen them the moment I'd walked through the door—they were large and elaborate and difficult to miss. So large, in fact, that a card had been easily lost between the stems. I reached in carefully and pulled it out.

The envelope was made from a thick cream card-stock, and the inside was lined with silver. A smooth piece of stationery was tucked inside and folded in half. I slid it out carefully and read the enclosed letter.

Phineas

Usually it is the woman being wooed with flowers. Usually it is the man chasing after the woman. Our relationship is not very usual.

I know you are upset with me because of my outburst, but I won't apologize for my feelings. You may have enough women to keep you company that you don't need me any longer, but you are all I have. Forgive me and things can be as they once were. Forgive me, and we can be happy again.

I've attached the watch you pointed to that afternoon we spent together the last time you were in London. It never suited my husband, but I suspect the snake will suit you just fine. Wear it and think of me.

Cornelia H.

ONCE I PUT the letter away in the envelope, I noticed a silky ribbon wrapped around the narrowest part of the vase. There was a kink in the ribbon where it had been knotted tightly, and it looked like it had once been tied around a small object. Perhaps, the watch mentioned in the letter.

I searched the entire room on my hands and knees for the watch with a snake on it, but I couldn't find it anywhere. It was possible the police had taken it, though if they had, they likely would have taken the letter, as well. Unless, of course, they hadn't seen the letter and had simply found the watch lying on the desk where Phineas may have left it.

It didn't matter, anyway. I didn't need the watch to prove anything. I knew who the letter was from.

My mother spoke poorly of Lady Cornelia Haddington. She had for years. No one in their social circle cared for her or her husband much. When he died, the funeral was poorly attended. Even my mother, usually the first one to sacrifice in the name of propriety, made her excuses and stayed home.

Lord Haddington had possessed a bad reputation and, it was whispered, even had connections with a criminal element here in town. Because of my mother's protectiveness, I didn't know much about the details beyond that. She simply spoke of Lord and Lady Haddington as though they were not to be trusted.

Phineas St. Clair must have felt differently, however. Lady Haddington wrote as though they'd once been quite close, spending days together in her empty mansion now that her husband had passed on and she had no children. Prior to the death of her husband, I heard her joke once that she didn't need children because her fortune would keep her company. Apparently, her riches had proven poor company if she was writing such a desperate letter to Phineas St. Clair.

What outburst had she been referring to? And was she trying to send a message with the snake watch? Perhaps, calling Phineas a snake for his untrustworthiness?

The rumor mill churned with the knowledge that Phineas St. Clair had a woman in every major city, but how many of those women were aware they weren't his sole focus? How many of them were disturbed by that?

And how many of them were vindictive enough to do something about it?

Lord Haddington had criminal connections. Was it possible Lady Haddington had tapped into them to exact revenge? It seemed elaborate, though certainly not impossible. People had been killed for reasons far more trivial than love.

I was still crouched on the floor next to the coffee table, staring at the flowers as though the answers to my question could be found there, when the door to the dressing room opened.

I jolted to my feet in an attempt to look like I belonged there, but it only served to make me look guilty. Thankfully, I recognized the pale face staring back at me from the door.

"Miss Beckingham?" Judith asked, her brow furrowed. She pushed the door open wide. "What are you doing in here?"

"I thought this was Phineas St. Clair's dressing room," I said, avoiding her question with an innocuous statement.

"It is. Well, *was*," she said. "I'm here to prepare the room for Alfred. Now that he will be taking the lead role, the dressing room will be his."

"That seems quick."

"It's business," she said with a shrug.

She was right, of course. It wasn't as though Phineas lived in the room. All of the actors stayed at the hotel next door. The dressing rooms were just for preparing before the shows and for taking breaks during rehearsals. It was probably why the room was so bare. The watch I had spent ten minutes looking for was more than likely in Phineas' luggage back at the hotel, which was probably on its way back to his grieving family.

"I thought you worked for the costume department," I said.

"I do," Judith said a little defensively. "But Alfred wanted someone he trusts to prepare his room, and I'm happy to help him. He is a good man."

I nodded. I had no opinion on Alfred. The only time I'd met him, he'd yelled at me for being backstage. He had a point, of course, since I'd been spying on the corpse of his fellow actor, but the entire experience had colored my opinion of him nonetheless.

"Why are you in here?" Judith asked again.

I wouldn't be able to sidestep my way out of the question, so I quickly flipped through my options.

I could tell Judith the same thing I told Rosalie—that I was investigating the death privately for Mr. Williamson—but she had a direct connection back to my house. If Judith mentioned it to the housemaid Louise, there was a chance it could make it back to my parents and then Mr. Williamson, and I would have to explain my lies to everyone. That was not an option.

Then, I remembered what Rosalie had first thought when she'd seen me backstage, and it seemed like as good an excuse as any.

"Phineas and I were...involved," I said, feeling guilty for the lie. The only person who could deny it was no longer alive to do so, and he apparently had enough women in his life that no one would question one more. Still, it felt wrong to lie about something as personal as his romantic life. "I just wanted to come here and...say goodbye."

Judith's face crumpled in concern. She pouted out her lower lip and nodded. "I'm sorry, Miss Beckingham. I had no idea. I'm sure Alfred wouldn't have treated you the way he did last night if he'd known. Why didn't you say anything then?"

"Shock." I shrugged. "I didn't really believe it yet."

"I understand." Judith stepped into the room, pushing the door half-closed behind her for a small amount of privacy. "May I be frank?"

"Of course." I would love nothing more than if everyone would be frank all the time. It would certainly make my investigations easier.

"You are better off without a man like Phineas St. Clair. I know that is a horrible thing to say after what has happened to him, but..." She shrugged like she couldn't help but speak the truth. "He used women for what they could give him and nothing more. He may have meant something to you, but I can assure you, you didn't mean much to him."

Had I actually been in love with Phineas St. Clair, Judith's words would have been crushing. I wanted to warn her to keep thoughts like that to herself, especially should she ever come in contact with a woman named Lady Haddington. Instead, I just nodded and thanked her for her honesty.

"A lot of actors are that way. Trust me," she said. "Though, not my Alfred."

"*Your* Alfred?"

Judith's pale face went pink.

"It sounds like you and Alfred have more than a business relationship," I prodded with a teasing smile.

She pressed a finger to her lips, shushing me, but her smile was apparent. Judith was in love.

"I hope so," she admitted. "He is a kind, talented man, and I'm very fond of him. Also, I know he is lonely. Travelling the way they do for these shows, he can't settle down the way any good man wants to."

"And what of you? Are you lonely?"

"I wouldn't mind his company if that is what you are asking," she said. "We both travel with the company, so we could make it work."

Her eyes went distant and dreamy, considering her possible future with Alfred Grey, and then all at once, Judith shook her head and stood tall.

"I've said too much," she said. "If any of this found its way back to Alfred, I would be mortified. He is a respected man, and I would hate for anyone to think that he is anything less than a professional. I shouldn't have—"

I reached out and laid a hand on the woman's shoulder. "I won't say anything. We can keep each other's secrets—mine about Phineas, and yours about Alfred."

She sighed with relief and nodded. "That would be nice."

"Good." I smoothed down my skirt and brushed dust from my knees where I'd crawled across the floor.

Judith cleared her throat. "I'm sorry, but I do still need to clean the room."

"Of course." I scooted past her to the door. "I'm sorry to keep you from your work."

Judith assured me I wasn't a disturbance, but she quickly closed the door as soon as I was in the hallway, and I could hear her humming to herself as she set to work getting rid of the last remnants of Phineas St. Clair's presence in the room.

7

I didn't run into anyone else as I left the backstage area and rejoined the general population of the theatre.

The lobby was much less filled than it had been prior to the tour. Saturday's matinee had been cancelled due to the death of the lead, so there wasn't much reason for anyone aside from employees and detectives to be there. And the tour was either still going on somewhere in the depths of the large building or it had ended while I was investigating Phineas' old dressing room.

I grabbed my coat from the coat closet, which was still unmanned, and buttoned it to the neck before pulling my cloche hat down over my ears and walking out into the brisk midday air. The sun was high in the sky, casting everything in a yellow glow and making it look warm, but a sharp breeze cut through the façade and made me cower inside my coat. I lowered my head—against the wind and the photographers who were still posted at the base of the stairs seeking statements from passersby—and gripped the iron railing as I descended the stairs.

I planned to find Louise as soon as I got home. Although I'd just spoken with Judith, I had the feeling she was more reserved with me than she would be with her own family. If she had any secret knowledge about Phineas St. Clair or anyone else in the company, I wanted to know about it, and Louise didn't strike me as the type to guard a secret.

Before I even reached the bottom of the stairs, I heard someone say my name. Assuming it was a journalist who recognized me from the days when my family's scandal dominated the papers, I lifted a dismissive hand and kept walking.

Suddenly, fingers wrapped around mine. Not aggressively, but tenderly. Still, I startled at the unexpected contact and spun around to find Sherborne Sharp smiling down at me.

He looked like a standing shadow, stretched tall and clad in dark blue with a hat to match. It was as if he'd been peeled up off the ground from behind some businessman and planted on his feet to walk amongst the humans. I had to take a step back to properly look up into his face, but Sherborne still held onto my hand.

"Is that how you greet a friend?" he teased, tipping his head towards my hand.

I yanked it back and smoothed down my coat, though it didn't need smoothing. "Is that how you treat a lady?" I fired back, eyebrow raised in a challenge.

"My apologies. I didn't mean to frighten you."

"You didn't," I said quickly. My heart was still fluttering nervously in my chest. "Why are you here? Are you following me?"

"Why would I be following you?" he asked coyly.

"I'm certain I don't know. That is why I asked you."

He smiled and sighed. "I didn't follow you here, but I did come here to wait for you."

I shook my head. "You aren't making sense. How did you know I was inside?"

"Your maid, Louise. I went to your house to see you, and she answered the door. She was more than happy to tell me your exact location without even the slightest bit of prompting."

Well, that proved my theory that Louise was not one to keep secrets. I would have to be careful with how I questioned her. I wouldn't want her spilling the details of my investigation to anyone else, especially Judith.

"Louise told me you came to the theatre for a tour," Sherborne said, looking up at the building with disbelief written plainly across his face. "But considering the events of last night, I suspected you had other motives for being here."

"The owner himself invited me last night," I said. "It would have been rude to decline his invitation."

"I'm sure the owner has more pressing matters on his mind now," Sherborne said.

"Why did you come to my house at all?"

He pressed his mouth into a flat, disapproving line. "Because the moment I read the newspaper, I knew you would involve yourself in this matter somehow."

I hated the way he spoke of me. Like I was a child dabbling in the affairs of adults. Like a mischievous nuisance.

I crossed my arms over my chest and lifted my chin. "I did not *involve* myself in anything. I was at the theatre last night when the incident occurred."

Sherborne's eyes widened in surprise, and then narrowed. "You mean when the accident occurred?"

"Accident, incident." I shrugged. "Call it what you like."

He lowered his head and pressed his fingertips to his forehead.

"Headache?" I asked, mock concern painted on my face. "You should go home and rest if you aren't feeling well."

"With you in my life, Alice, I'm afraid I may never feel well again."

I looked away from him, sighing in a bored kind of way. "Anyway, if you only came here to tell me to mind my business, then you'll be happy to know I am doing just that. Perhaps, you should try it."

He frowned like he didn't understand me.

"No one has instructed you to keep watch over me, Mr. Sharp. There is no need to come to my house and track me around the city worrying over me. I am not in your charge."

"As I already said, there was no tracking involved. You should speak with your maid about how freely she shares your whereabouts. It is dangerous."

"Louise is not a threat to my safety. She only told you because she knows we are friends and, truthfully, she would tell you anything you wanted to know. She is quite fond of you."

It was true enough. Recently, Sherborne had made one or two discreet visits to the house to bring me information, and some of the servants had taken a liking to him. Still, as I watched a self-satisfied smile spread across his face, I wished I hadn't shared Louise's feelings with him. He did not need any more reason to feel superior.

"Louise is fond of most every man she meets. There is no need to feel special."

"You seem annoyed by the idea," Sherborne said, tipping his head to the side. "Is it because you are fond of me, too? Is that why you asked me to meet with you?"

My brow furrowed in confusion before I remembered what he was referring to. I had, indeed, sent for Sherborne. "That was days ago. So long ago I'd almost forgotten I asked you to come see me."

"As you've said, you are not in my charge. I had other matters to attend to and could not drop everything to rush to your side at first command. I came first thing this morning."

"You came because you thought I needed saving."

Sherborne smiled. "I thought I might be able to accomplish two tasks at once: answer your call and keep you out of trouble."

"Sorry to disappoint you, but I am perfectly fine. I wanted to speak with you about using your contacts to help me find some information."

"What kind of information?" he asked, shifting into his business voice.

I tried to speak as calmly as possible, as though the information hardly mattered. "I want to know of the existence of a man who goes by the name 'The Chess Master.' Or, perhaps, *went* by that name. He might very well be dead."

If Rose was telling me the truth, The Chess Master

was lying at the bottom of the Thames. That didn't mean there wouldn't still be people who recognized that name or people who knew about his schemes while he had been alive. Even if The Chess Master was dead, someone might be able to tell me how he and my brother were connected; whether The Chess Master was responsible for Edward's murder in prison.

The teasing smile that had been playing at the sides of Sherborne's mouth since his arrival faded entirely. He frowned, a crease forming between his eyebrows, and crossed his arms. "Why would he be dead?"

"Because people die. It is the unfortunate way of the world, as we both know."

His frown deepened. "What are you involved in, Alice?"

"Nothing," I said honestly. I wanted to be involved, but with Catherine and Rose both staying tight-lipped, I didn't have enough information. Hopefully, Sherborne could help me with that. "Truly, it is nothing. I just need some information."

"Just information?" he clarified. "You don't need anything else from me?"

"Nothing else."

Suddenly, I couldn't tell whether it was disapproval I was seeing on Sherborne's face or disappointment. "Fine. I'll do what I can, but I would regret it if I did not warn you—"

I held up a finger to pause him. "Careful. You might live to regret it if you do warn me about whatever it is you are going to say."

"I'm not afraid of you, Miss Beckingham," he said, his eyes sparkling with mischief. "I simply want to warn you not to involve yourself in the death of Phineas St. Clair. I've seen you investigate several deaths now, and despite appearances, I do trust your judgment. However, this case is not the death of an old family friend. Phineas St. Clair was a world-recognized actor. This matter is bigger than the both of us, and I don't want to see you get yourself hurt."

The memory of Sherborne Sharp saving me during my last altercation with a murderer rose to the forefront of my mind, and I had to assume it was in his thoughts, as well. Sherborne had saved my life and that was a debt I would not be able to repay. Still, it did not give him any kind of control over my life or what I did with it.

"Luckily, the matter of my safety is not your concern. Even if it was, you have nothing to worry about. The only thing I'm asking you to do is seek out the information I've requested. You will be compensated, of course."

"I do not want your money, Alice."

His admission surprised me, and when I looked up at him, his eyes were downturned and thoughtful.

"That is your choice."

"It is," he said in agreement, taking a deep breath and rising to his full height. He offered his elbow to me. "Would you like for me to escort you home?"

"Have you not understood the point of this conversation?" I teased. "I do not need you to worry about me."

"I am not offering because I'm worried about you. I'm offering because I am a gentleman."

A burst of laughter shot out of me. "That is news to me."

Before I could decline his offer, I once again heard my name called. Sherborne and I both turned to look up the stairs as Thomas came bounding down them, his hat pressed to his chest. When he reached us, he was quite out of breath, his tan face flushed with exertion.

"I have been looking all over for you. I thought for certain you had already left."

"I nearly had, except I ran into an old friend. This is Sherborne Sharp."

Thomas extended his hand in greeting, and Sherborne stared at it for a second before gripping it firmly and giving the man one quick shake. Thomas flexed his fingers after letting go.

"I met Thomas during the tour," I explained.

"Yes, she kept me from falling over with boredom," Thomas said warmly. "Except there at the end. Where did you get to? I couldn't find you for the rest of the tour."

I felt Sherborne's eyes on me. He knew me well enough to be more suspicious than Thomas was.

"Another engagement," I said. "I had to meet with someone."

"Who?" Sherborne asked, eyes narrowed.

I kept my expression neutral, though my eyes were piercing. "A lady must maintain an air of mystery, Mr. Sharp. Otherwise, she risks seeming boring."

"No one would dare accuse you of such a thing," Thomas said.

"Indeed not," Sherborne agreed.

I was quite ready to be done with both men at that point and would have felt no guilt at all for excusing myself and leaving them to an awkward goodbye.

"Well, I actually need to be going," I started.

"Wait a moment," Thomas said. "I was looking for

you because I wanted to know if you planned to come to tomorrow's matinee showing."

"Oh. Well, I guess I hadn't thought about it."

"Would you like to think about it?" Thomas asked. "That is, would you like to attend with me? Since we made it through the tour together, I thought it might be nice to experience the show together, as well."

Sherborne shifted from foot to foot like the ground was boiling beneath him.

"I could be persuaded," I admitted. Especially since going to a showing of the play would give me another reason to be back at the theatre. A lot seemed to be happening inside its walls and it seemed important to my investigation to be nearby lest anything important be discovered. I had more questions than answers about Judith, Alfred Grey, and the rest of the cast.

"Then let me persuade you," Thomas said, grinning from ear to ear. "Meet me here tomorrow afternoon an hour before showtime?"

"Certainly. Yes. That would be lovely."

Thomas seemed pleased as he donned his hat, wished us farewell, and headed off down the street. Sherborne, staring after him with a frown, seemed less happy. When he turned back to me, it looked like he had smelled something particularly unpleasant.

"You just met that man?"

"Inside during the tour, yes. He is very friendly."

"He is a stranger," he said. "Should you really be going out with a strange man you just met?"

"We are meeting in a public location," I said, rolling my eyes. "Besides, there you go worrying about me again. It is a habit you really ought to break."

"I'll do my best." He sighed. Then, he extended his elbow once again. "Shall we?"

I patted his arm and pointed to the corner where George sat in the car waiting for me. "We shall not. I'm sorry, but I've already arranged transport home."

"Excellent," Sherborne said drily. "Saves me the trouble."

"The trouble?" I asked as we both walked down the block toward the car. "I thought you were a gentleman. Wouldn't it have been your pleasure?"

"Actions make a man a gentleman," he said. "Not his feelings about those actions. I would have seen you safely home out of duty."

George opened the back door of the car for me, and I turned to face Sherborne. "Well, I'm glad you didn't have to be inconvenienced by concerns for my safety. Thank you for seeing me to the car, and do get in touch when you have pertinent information."

His mouth pressed into a line so thin I thought it might disappear altogether. Then, he tipped his hat to me and clipped down the block and around the corner at a quick pace, disappearing before George could even close the car door.

8

M y parents were in the sitting room when I got home, and my mother called my name immediately.

"I thought you would be gone," I said, hanging up my coat and going in to see them.

"We thought we would be, as well," my mother said crossly. "The event was meant to benefit that orphanage just across from the church. I don't remember the name, but it was for the children. Put on by Lady Haddington, if you can believe it."

"Lady Haddington?" I asked, surprised to hear the name for the second time that day.

"Exactly," my mother said. "No one would have ever accused her of being charitable, but she suddenly caught the spirit and wanted to host a fundraiser. Except, she had to cancel at the last minute. She sent out notifications to half of the guests this morning, but we were not fortunate enough to receive one before getting dressed in our finest and traveling across town."

"Why did she cancel?"

My mother shrugged. "Had I received notice from her, I might know. As it is, I only know she cancelled due to emotional distress, and I wasted a perfectly good morning."

"We can still have a perfectly good afternoon," my father said in a monotone attempt to comfort her.

Could Lady Haddington's cancellation have anything to do with Phineas St. Clair? It had to. It would be more surprising if the two events weren't related at all.

"You don't seem concerned about her emotional distress," I said.

"That is because I'm not," my mother said. "That woman lives to be the center of attention. I wouldn't be surprised if she planned the entire benefit with the intention of cancelling at the last moment. Now, people will drop by her house and worry over her, and she'll get to look charitable while really, she is a selfish—"

"Eleanor," my father said, cutting her off.

My mother took a deep breath. "I'm sorry. I'm just upset. Not only because of Lady Haddington, but because of my bracelet. Do you know the gold bracelet I had on last night, Alice? The one Catherine gave me for my birthday last year?"

I nodded. Catherine had refused to tell me what she was getting Mama for a gift because she wanted her gift to outshine all of the others. Perhaps, my sister and Lady Haddington would have something in common in that regard. I'd ended up giving Mama a crystal paperweight that sat on the shelf in Papa's library, and Catherine had given her a beautiful golden bracelet that she wore more often than not.

"Well, it's gone."

"What do you mean?" I asked.

"I can't find it." Mama threw up her arms in desperation. "I've searched the entire house—"

"She had the maids search the entire house," my father quietly corrected.

"I can't find it anywhere. I had it on last night when we left for the theatre, but now it is gone. I must have dropped it in all of the chaos while getting outside."

I didn't see how the rush outside would have affected the clasp on her bracelet, but my thoughts were still stuck on Lady Haddington and her reason for cancelling her event.

"Did you see an area for people to report lost and found articles while you were at the theatre today?" Mama asked. "Perhaps, I should have George drive me down there. I could ask around and see if anyone has seen it."

"I'll look for you when I go tomorrow."

"Tomorrow?" my mother asked, brows furrowed. "Why are you going back to the theatre tomorrow?"

"For the matinee performance."

"By yourself?" she asked. "Would you like us to go with you? I wouldn't want you to go alone."

"No, I will have company. I met the lead actress today, and she invited the tour group to come to the performance."

I could have told my mother about Thomas and his offer, but I did not want her to think it a romantic engagement. She would have been much too excited about the prospect, and there seemed no reason to rile her for what would ultimately amount to nothing.

"I don't think I could force myself to walk back into that building," my mother said with a shudder. "At least not for this play. I'm surprised they didn't cancel the entire show."

I did not press my mother to overcome her fears because the farther she stayed from the theatre, the easier my investigation would be.

Shortly after arriving, I excused myself to the kitchen to find some lunch.

I planned to find Louise after eating and talk with her, but when I walked into the kitchen, she was standing at the sink scrubbing furiously at a towel under the cold water. She started when the kitchen door swung open.

"Miss Beckingham," she said, eyes going wide as she looked from me to the towel and back again.

There was a large black stain across the center of the towel that didn't seem to be improved by Louise's attempts to clean it.

"There was a spill in the study, and I grabbed something to mop it up before any of your father's papers could be ruined, but in the process, I ruined a towel. I wasn't thinking," she said, out of breath. "Your mother will be unhappy, so I thought I'd try to correct it before telling her—"

"No need to tell her," I said, plucking the towel out of Louise's hands and dropping it in the rubbish bin under the counter.

"Not tell her?" she asked, her freckled face wrinkled in confusion.

"I'll say it was my fault," I offered. "She'll be upset with me, but not inordinately so."

Louise shook her head. "Why would you do that, Miss?"

The fear in Louise's eyes made her look younger. Her face was pale, her freckles standing out even more than usual, and her eyes were wide and frantic.

"I must admit, my kindness does not come freely. I'm hoping to gather some information from you."

Louise glanced at the stained towel in the bin again and then, determining my offer was better than having to face my mother's wrath, she nodded. "Of course. Anything."

"We spoke briefly of your cousin this morning. Judith?"

She nodded.

"Well, I wondered how much you might know of Judith's time spent with the touring company? Travelling with a group of famous actors must bring with it a lot of interesting stories, and I am interested to know what she has seen and heard."

Louise lit up, clearly thrilled that gossip was my price for taking the blame for her mistake. "Judith and I write to one another all the time. Our mothers remained very close throughout our childhoods, so she has always been more like a sister to me than a cousin. When she left to tour with the theatre company, I have to admit I almost died with jealousy. She tried to get me a position with them, too, but no one needed anything cleaned or tidied."

Her mouth turned down in bitterness for a moment before she refocused on the task at hand. "What is it you want to know?"

"Well, she worked in close contact with Phineas St.

Clair before his death. Did she ever say what that was like?"

"I'm afraid you might not like what Judith had to say," Louise admitted. "She said that Phineas St. Clair was not the man he made himself out to be in public. Everyone counted him amongst the rich and famous, but as it turns out, he may have just been famous. Judith said that he put himself on the arm of wealthy widows in every city so they could shower him with gifts and fine dining he wouldn't otherwise be able to afford."

I frowned. "But he was paid by the theatre company for his performances. How could he not have any money of his own?"

Louise shrugged. "All I know is by the last night of shows in every city, the theatres would nearly have to bar the doors to keep away all of the women who felt they'd been cheated by Phineas. One night, a woman threatened his life if he didn't return the money she had given him, and the director took it so seriously that he put the understudy on in Phineas' stead."

"Alfred Grey?" I asked.

"Judith would be thrilled to hear that you know his name," Louise said. "She writes of Alfred constantly. She hasn't come right out and said so, but I know she is hopelessly in love with the man. She speaks endlessly about his superior talent, but everyone was so busy fawning over Phineas that they never paid him any mind. I suppose that will change now that Alfred will be taking over the lead."

"Yes, I suppose it will," I said, the loose threads in my mind beginning to connect.

"Alfred was given two shows a week, but Phineas

thought even that was too many. The night Alfred was put on instead of him, Judith said that Phineas nearly quit the entire play. It took the director and Rosalie Stuart talking to him for over an hour before he agreed to let Alfred perform for him that night and stay with the company."

"Did Phineas just not like sharing the spotlight?" I asked.

"Judith claimed it was about the money. When Alfred went on instead of Phineas on the nights Phineas was supposed to perform, Phineas' cut of the profits went to Alfred. And if Judith was telling the truth about his finances, he didn't have the money to lose." Louise sighed and shook her head. "Alfred just liked to perform. He didn't want to take any money from Phineas, but their relationship still fractured after that night. Judith said that things were tense backstage. Phineas snapped at the crew and would push himself almost to ruin when he was ill rather than take a night off and allow Alfred to take over the role for the evening. Judith told me Alfred had discussed leaving the company and taking a role somewhere else simply because the emotional toll was too much for him. She convinced him to stay."

"How?" I asked, wondering what a costumer's assistant like Judith could have said to Alfred Grey to convince him to do anything. Based on the conversation I'd had with her earlier in the day, she and Alfred were not in a romantic relationship. She didn't even want it getting out that she admired him. So, what could she have said to convince him to stay with the company?

Louise opened her mouth just as my mother's voice rang through the house.

"Louise?"

The maid stiffened and looked at me, wide-eyed. "I should go."

I grabbed her arm just as she turned away. "Could you let me know if Judith says anything else to you?"

"About Phineas?" Louise asked, brow furrowed.

"About anything at all," I said. "This has been a very interesting conversation."

She smiled, momentarily proud until my mother called for her again, and she shrank down into herself and hurried from the kitchen.

Alone, I leaned against the counter and crossed my arms. I had a lot of information to digest.

Phineas St. Clair may have been poor. He used women and treated his cast mates and crew poorly. No one—aside from his adoring admirers—seemed very fond of him. The question seemed to be not whether or not Phineas was killed, but by whom?

9

A fter an afternoon of grumbling about Lady Haddington's last-minute cancellation and the waste of a good dress, my father caught the hint and took my mother out for a night on the town. They planned to go for dinner and dancing, which further proved how much my father was trying to please my mother. He hated dancing. Still, he seemed in good spirits when they left, and my mother was so excited she didn't worry at all about leaving me home alone.

With the house to myself, I combed through the collection of old newspapers in my father's study. He liked to keep the papers for the last month next to his desk so he could look at the fluctuation in the stock market. I was only grateful he kept the entire paper. It meant I had an entire month worth of articles promoting the newest play starring Phineas St. Clair and Rosalie Stuart.

Many of the articles focused on the details of the touring dates and the availability of tickets, but a few of them branched out to include bits of information about the stars.

> *Phineas St. Clair portrays Richard, the male lead who connives his way into high-society along with his wife, Victoria. This role requires a good deal of acting on St. Clair's part, as he was born into wealth. Despite his family's successful business, St. Clair chose to make his own fortune in the theatre. It seems to have been a good choice for the gifted young actor.*

Another article, one published the day before Phineas St. Clair's death, discussed his first night in London.

> *The cast of* To the Top *has arrived in London, and the lead actor, Phineas St. Clair, is already making his presence known. He was seen having dinner at a recently-opened restaurant near the West End with one lady, and then spotted several hours later with another. His reputation as a ladies' man preceded his arrival, but he seems intent on cementing it as fact.*

How many of Phineas' girlfriends read that same article? Lady Haddington, perhaps? It would explain the flowers and gift she'd sent him, along with the slightly aggressive note. She'd mentioned his large collection of women. Maybe her jealousy had been stoked by the article about his arrival and his failure to visit her immediately upon arriving in the city. And maybe her "emotional distress" had little to do with his death, but was instead caused by her own broken heart over his rejection.

It was all just a theory, but a probable one given what Judith had told Louise about the threats Phineas had received in the past from his scorned lovers.

I was still rifling through the stack of newspapers when Miller, our butler, stepped into the room to inform me that a man was at the front door.

"For me?" I asked. Unexpected guests were rare enough, let alone an unexpected guest there to see me. I left Miller to tidy my father's study back to its usual state and rushed downstairs to see who could be at the door.

I half-expected to find Sherborne Sharp there waiting for me, prepared to give me another lecture about keeping to myself and not involving myself in dangerous affairs. Instead, I was shocked to see the owner of The Royal Coliseum standing in my entrance hall, his bowler hat spinning nervously in his hands.

"Mr. Williamson," I said in greeting. I didn't know why he was there, and my heart rate kicked up in anticipation. "To what do I owe the pleasure?"

"Miss Alice," he said, lowering his head. "I'm sorry to intrude on your evening. I would have called ahead, but there wasn't time."

"A visit from a family friend is never an intrusion," I said. "If you wished to speak with my parents as well, I'm sure the butler told you they aren't here. They went out for the evening."

"All the better, actually," he said with a nervous smile. "I hoped to speak with you alone."

I led him to the sitting room, trying to hide the

surprise and confusion behind my hospitality. "Could I offer you tea or anything to eat?"

"No, no," he said, waving his hands in refusal. "I won't keep you long."

He sat in the center of the couch, the cushions on either side of him slanting under his weight. I claimed the chair usually reserved for my father.

"I won't delay any further," he said. "I came here because I've just spoken with Rosalie Stuart."

My rapidly beating heart seemed to freeze solid in my chest.

"And?" I said, feigning confusion. I'd told Rosalie Stuart that Mr. Williamson himself had asked me to investigate the murder. I'd lied to her, and she had told Mr. Williamson my lie. I'd been discovered, and this long-time friend of my parents was here to ban me from the theatre for life.

"She told me that she ran into you backstage, and you claimed to be there on my orders. She said you were investigating the death of Phineas St. Clair."

My cheeks felt boiling hot, and I knew I was red from head to toe. I was so mortified, my tongue felt swollen in my mouth, and I had to clear my throat several times before I could even speak.

"I'm so sorry, Mr. Williamson. I should not have lied to Rosalie, especially in regards to you. The truth is, she caught me backstage, and I—"

"Were you investigating the death?" he asked.

I debated lying again, but I didn't want to make things worse. So, I nodded.

"On whose orders?"

"My own," I said. "My parents always said I was too

curious, and I suppose I've proven them right. I understand if you are angry. I would be if the situation were reversed. I only hope—"

"I am not angry," he said, interrupting me. "In fact, I'm relieved someone was at least looking into the matter."

I blinked at him. "You are?"

"Yes," he said, sighing, his shoulders sagging forward. "The police have all but given up on the investigation, certain the death was an accident, and you can't imagine the trouble it has put me in. I've told them that those lights were inspected the day of the show, but they won't hear any other possibility. Not many people know this, but my theatre is in dangerous financial straits. I need every seat filled for every performance this year or I may not open next season."

"I'm so sorry, Mr. Williamson. I had no idea."

"Not many people do," he said again. "I would like it to stay that way if possible. I'm only confiding in you because you may be able to help me."

I still didn't fully understand what he was offering. "I don't quite see how."

He lowered his head, looking up at me from beneath his graying brows. "If people think the ceiling could come down on their heads, they won't come to the theatre. I need to prove that this was no accident."

"But what if it was an accident?" I had my suspicions that Phineas St. Clair had been targeted, but that did not make it true.

"Either way, both options deserve to be explored," he said. "And I know your cousin Rose and her husband run a successful detective agency. Your mother and father told me about it at dinner just last weekend."

"They do, but they are away on business right now. By the time they came here, it would be too late."

"I don't want them. I want you, Alice," he said, pointing at me to drive home his meaning. "As I said, I don't have the money to hire an outside agency right now or the time to devote to it, but clearly, the ability to solve puzzles runs in your family. I've heard rumors that you were involved in the investigation into Violet Colburn's death, and it seems that you conducted yourself sensibly and discreetly in that matter. You came to the theatre today to investigate the death of Phineas, and now I'm giving you my permission to do so on a more official basis."

I'd been awaiting the day that someone would take me seriously. I'd wanted nothing more than for people to respect my thoughts and feelings and opinions in a tangible way. Now, it had happened, and I felt like cowering in the corner.

"I am not a professional," I said. "I am merely interested in detective work. I don't think you should rest the fate of the theatre on my abilities."

"I trust your judgment," he said.

"Why?" It didn't make any sense. Mr. Williamson had known my family since I was a child, but he didn't know much about me. He had no reason to put his faith in me. Yet, he was.

"Aside from your experience in the Colburn murder? Because I know Achilles Prideaux's reputation and that of your cousin Rose. If you are even half as talented as they are, you'll have this case solved in a matter of days."

The trouble was, I didn't think I was half as talented as my cousin and her husband. Maybe not even a quarter as talented. I'd solved two cases when the victims were close friends of mine and the suspects were ordinary people, but this case involved well-recognized actors and actresses. When Sherborne had come to me earlier in the day to warn me, I'd found his worrying annoying and unnecessary, but now I couldn't help but wonder whether he hadn't made a fair point. I have no idea how to solve this mystery.

"Come to the theatre tomorrow before lunch," Mr. Williamson said, pressing his palms to his knees to lift himself to standing. "You don't have to decide now. Just come to the theatre and let me explain my side of the story more fully. If you still don't think you can help when it is all over, then I won't mention it again. Just take it into consideration."

Mr. Williamson's request was hard to deny. Especially since he seemed so desperate.

He'd looked frazzled when I saw him at the theatre that morning, but even in the less than twelve hours that had passed since then, he looked older, if that was possible. Thin lines webbed out from the corners of his eyes, and he seemed to have more gray speckled in his hair.

If nothing was done, his theatre could shutter its doors forever. That would not be my fault, but I would have a hard time convincing myself of that if I did nothing to help him.

So, despite Sherborne's advice to mind my own business ringing in my head, I assured Mr. Williamson that he would see me at the theatre tomorrow.

"Thank you, Alice," he said, grabbing my hand in a

firm shake before donning his hat. "You and I will make a great team, I'm sure of it. We will solve this case together and save my theatre."

I wanted to remind him that I hadn't agreed to take on the investigation yet, but he skipped out of the door before I could.

10

M y tour led by Mr. Williamson was much different than the one I'd experienced the day before. There were no interesting facts about the age of the building or the artists who painted the murals on the ceilings. Mr. Williams mentioned nothing of the world-famous actors and actresses who had graced the building and delivered great performances. Instead, he bypassed one-hundred years of history and focused on one actor on one day. Phineas St. Clair on the Friday previous.

"The director wanted to have a dress rehearsal that morning to ensure the sets and lighting would be ready for the inaugural performance that night," he said. "The cast and crew gathered just before lunch and ran through the play as fast as possible. Everything went off perfectly, and they broke for lunch."

"Did they eat here in the building?" I asked.

"Yes, we always have food brought in for the first day of the performance. Phineas St. Clair was there along with the rest of the cast and crew. Everyone seemed in good spirits when they left an hour later for their dressing rooms."

"Phineas stayed here in his dressing room? He didn't go back to the hotel?"

"Correct," Mr. Williamson said, scrunching up his forehead to help him remember all of the details of the dead actor's movements on his final day. "Rosalie Stuart left just after lunch, though I'm not sure where she went, but everyone else stayed here in the building. There was a lot of unpacking and setting up to be done, so most everyone helped with that process."

"Phineas helped unpack?"

"No," he said with a bitter laugh and a shake of his head. "Sorry. No, he didn't. Most actors don't help with that kind of thing. They can, of course, and it is good for morale amongst the crew and my permanent staff at the theatre when they do, but most often they hide away in their rooms to focus on their performance. That was the decision Phineas St. Clair made."

"All right," I said, nodding, trying to pretend that any of this information was helping me to puzzle together what had happened. It wasn't, but I hoped eventually something would click into place. The more information I had, the better I could determine who had the motive and opportunity to murder the actor. "I'd assume the backstage area is very busy during the unloading process?"

"During the entire first day, really," Mr. Williamson said. We'd reached the front of the theatre, and he offered me his hand as he helped me up the stairs and onto the main stage. I could still see the dent in the wood where the light had fallen and crushed Phineas St. Clair two nights ago. The wood would have to be replaced if they hoped to get rid of it. I thought they should. It was difficult to look at the spot, knowing what had happened there.

Mr. Williamson made a sweeping gesture from the left side of the stage to the right. "People were bringing in the sets, configuring the lighting, and organizing the props. All hands were on deck for most of the day."

I twisted my mouth to one side. Anyone could have tampered with the light. If that many people were back here working, no one would have noticed if someone shimmied up the stairs and rigged up a light to fall.

"When was the equipment inspected?" I asked.

"One hour before showtime," he said quickly, as though he'd answered that question before. I suspected he had. Several times, in fact. "We always wait until the incoming company has set up the stage to their specifications before we inspect. It is our last assurance that we've taken care of any problems on our end and any malfunctions are not our fault. Of course, that thinking didn't get me very far in this case, but it is meant to be the purpose."

I looked up at the gap in the rigging where the missing light was supposed to be hung. "So, if someone tampered with the light, it would have to have been within that hour before showtime?"

He nodded. "Yes. Sometime between our inspection and curtain call."

"Would it be possible for someone to do that without being noticed?"

"One hour before curtain?" Mr. Williamson asked,

eyebrows raised. "Excuse me, Miss Alice, but someone could have danced across the stage in their undergarments, and I'm not sure anyone would have looked up. Backstage is a mess before curtain on opening night. Anyone could have done anything."

Mr. Williamson didn't know the exact movements of the rest of the cast and crew during the several hours before showtime, and I couldn't blame him. I'd seen him moments before the play started, and he had been frantic with last minute preparations. He'd been so busy making sure everything went perfectly that he was too busy to notice that something horrible was happening.

"Oh, there was one large problem that afternoon," he said, lifting his finger into the air. "Phineas' costume didn't fit."

"His costume?" I asked. "The one he'd been wearing throughout the entire tour?"

He nodded. "He tried it on after the dress rehearsal and the trousers were an inch too short and the shirt had been hemmed in so his buttons nearly popped free. He couldn't even fit inside."

"How did that happen?"

"A mix-up in the costume department, I suppose. The costume designer was on the verge of tears because she was so distressed over the mistake. Apparently, both costumes had been hemmed to the size specifications of the understudy by mistake. It happened sometime between the last performance at the previous theatre and the first one here. The director said the understudy should take Phineas' place for the night until the costume could be redone, but Phineas refused. He worked with the costume designer to loosen the seams and temporarily let out his clothes in strategic places so they wouldn't rip open on stage."

"Wouldn't it have been easier to just let the under-study take the stage?" I asked.

Mr. Williamson shrugged. "It certainly would have been easier for Phineas St. Clair. He might be alive right now if he'd agreed to the switch. I know Alfred has taken the reality of that particularly hard."

I remembered Alfred whispering with Judith the night of the accident. Standing ten paces away from the place where, had Phineas agreed to it, Alfred could have been lying dead beneath a light, Alfred smiled. He certainly hadn't seemed to be taking it hard that night, though I could not account for what shock could make a person do. Maybe the reality hadn't sunk in yet.

Mr. Williamson continued the tour of backstage. He said that the police were able to locate three of the four screws from the light scattered around the stage, proving the theory that the light had fallen rather than been tampered with because, in the words of the police: "if the light had been rigged to fall, there would be missing screws."

"There were missing screws," Mr. Williamson said exasperatedly. "There is still one screw no one has found."

I looked around the stage, at the large amount of space draped with curtains and ropes and sand bags, drenched in darkness. It seemed highly probable that a single screw could go missing. That it could roll into the cracks between boards and disappear forever.

Mr. Williamson directed the tour down the hallway that ran behind the stage where the dressing rooms were located. He pointed out Phineas St. Clair's previous room, which now had Alfred Grey's name written on a piece of paper taped next to the door.

"This was Phineas' room, but it has now been given to Alfred," he explained. "I would let you inside, but that would be an invasion of privacy."

"Actually," I said, slightly ashamed, "I already inspected Mr. St. Clair's room before it was given to Alfred. That is when I saw Rosalie backstage."

Mr. Williamson smiled in amusement and shook his head. "I might have guessed as much."

"While I was in there, I found a vase of flowers left for Phineas. Do you have any idea when that would have been delivered?"

Mr. Williamson frowned. "The mail is delivered mid-morning, so it probably would have been in his room upon his arrival unless it was brought in by special delivery. I remember seeing it in his room the night of the accident, so I know it was in there before he took the stage."

Phineas had definitely received the note and the watch before his death, then. But if he didn't go back to his hotel room at all that day, the watch should have been in his dressing room. I didn't think he'd have worn such an audacious piece of jewelry out on stage. Not if the costume department had anything to say about it.

"Do the flowers have anything to do with the case?" he asked.

"Not the flowers, per se, but the card and gift that went with them," I said.

He frowned. "Card?"

"It was tucked inside the flowers and mentioned a

watch that had been sent with it. I didn't find the watch during my search of the room, so I hoped to find out where it went. Maybe finding it would provide some answers about where Phineas went and who he spoke to in the last hours of his life."

"You think the watch could point to his murderer?" Mr. Williamson asked, his face going pale at the thought.

He had asked me here to help with the investigation, but I wondered whether he'd actually thought murder was a possibility or if he'd just hoped I could prove it wasn't his fault. The idea of murder disturbed him enough that I assumed the latter.

"Perhaps," I said. "Anything can be a clue. Do you have any idea what could have happened to something like that?"

He pulled at the tight collar of his shirt like the hallway was suddenly stuffy. "You would have to talk with the costume department. They manage all clothes and jewelry for all of the performers. If someone found it, they may have assumed it was a prop and taken it back there. Though, they deal with so many different wardrobes, it would be a miracle to find something as small as a watch, I'm sure."

"I should at least look into the possibility."

"Does that mean I have succeeded in persuading you to investigate the death?" he asked.

I smiled and shrugged. "I suppose it does. Maybe solving puzzles really does run in my family. I can't seem to stay away. For the time being, I'll do what I can to help, but I don't want to make any promises. Like I said, I'm not a professional."

"That is perfectly fine," he said. "I'd rather have

someone I know looking into it than a strange detective anyway. I trust you, Alice."

I smiled at his kindness and set out for the costume department. I'd only taken a few steps when Mr. Williamson stopped me.

"You said there was a card with the flowers. If the watch could be a clue, is there any way the person who sent the flowers could be involved?" he asked.

"I already thought of that, and I'm looking into it," I said. "From what I hear, Mr. St. Clair had a large group of admirers he knew personally. Any one of them could have been upset with the attention he divided amongst so many different women and tried to exact retribution."

Mr. Williamson bobbed his head back and forth, as if unsure. "It would have been difficult for anyone off the street to slip backstage without me noticing. I'd be surprised. Who sent the flowers? Maybe I know them."

"I'm sure you do," I said. Mr. Williamson moved in the same social circles as my mother, which meant he also moved in the same circles as Lady Haddington. He knew the woman, so it seemed inconsiderate to name her as a possible suspect with so little evidence.

He lowered his head, looking up at me from beneath his brows. "If you are worried about me saying anything, I can assure you I won't. I simply want to know who I should be looking out for. If this person comes to the theatre again, I want to know who they are so I can keep an eye on them.

I twisted my mouth to one side, unsure. He made a good point. As the owner of the theatre, Mr. Williamson deserved to know if a possible murderer was walking around backstage. So, I sighed and leaned in, my voice lower.

"The flowers and gift were from Lady Haddington."

Mr. Williamson jolted back as though he had been slapped, and all of the color drained from his face. I knew he would be surprised, but I hadn't expected him to be so dismayed.

"Did she send it as an admirer of his acting or—?"

"She appeared to have been in a romantic relationship with him," I admitted. "The letter spoke of a previous meeting they'd had the last time he was in London. She seemed distressed that he was speaking with other women."

Mr. Williamson stared at my mouth blankly, blinking slowly as the reality of my words sank in.

I knew he deserved to know, but everyone already thought poorly enough about Lady Haddington, that I felt guilty for adding more fuel to that fire. "The relationship was clearly supposed to remain private, so I'm sure she wouldn't want anyone to know. I am no gossip, and I wouldn't have even told you, except you are the owner, so—"

"I won't tell," he said in an emotionless voice. "Thank you for the information, Alice."

Before I could say anything else, Mr. Williamson turned on his heel and marched dazedly down the hallway in the direction of the stage.

∿

WITHOUT MR. WILLIAMSON'S HELP, I found the costume department. It was at the end of the hallway, past the dressing rooms. A large room with low ceilings and no windows, stuffed to overflowing with racks of clothes, reams of fabric, and wooden boxes of thread, buttons, zippers, and anything else a costumer could ever dream of having.

Sitting in the middle of the mess was a gray-haired woman who was studying a suit hanging from a mannequin with narrowed eyes.

She was so focused on her work, she didn't immediately notice when I walked through the door. I had to clear my throat twice before she looked away from the suit. Even then, it took several seconds for her eyes to focus on me.

"Who are you?" she asked.

"Alice Beckingham." She reminded me of my nanny as a child. A woman who commanded respect and would settle for nothing less. I knew how to handle her. "I'm sorry to intrude on your work. I know it is very important."

She nodded at the compliment, clearly agreeing with me, and then leaned away from the suit, slouching down in her chair. "I'm in need of a break, anyway. How can I help you?"

For someone whose job it was to dress people, her clothes seemed surprisingly uninteresting. She wore a dark gray dress that hung shapelessly around her wide hips and matching gray shoes with a low heel.

"I was brought in by Mr. Williamson, the owner—"

"I know who he is," she said, cutting me off.

"Of course," I said with a smile. "Well, Mr. Williamson brought me in to look into the matter of Phineas St. Clair's death."

The woman's brow wrinkled. "I thought the police were investigating that crime. They came in to speak with me already."

"I am not with the police. I am working...privately." The word 'unofficially' also came to mind, but I didn't want the woman to know I was as inexperienced as I actually was.

"Just like I told the police, I don't have much to say," she said. "On the day of the accident, I spent the hours before curtain resizing Phineas St. Clair's costume so he could wear it on stage. When that was finished, I collapsed in a chair and didn't get up until the news of the accident reached me."

"I don't need a statement from you. Actually, I need your permission to look through your jewelry."

She tilted her head to the side. "Are you looking for anything in particular?"

"A watch with a snake on it," I said. I still did not know whether the snake would be on the wrist strap or on the face of the watch. I didn't know exactly what I was looking for, but I had never seen a man's watch with a snake on it before, so I hoped I would know the right watch when I saw it. "I believe it belonged to Phineas St. Clair."

The woman shrugged. "I never saw him wear a watch like that, but you are welcome to look. Make sure things stay in the boxes they are in. I have them labeled to make things easy to find."

I agreed and began my search. The costumer showed me to an entire shelf of jewelry. It was a wooden dresser with wide, shallow drawers, inside of which jewelry was laid out meticulously. Many of the pieces were strapped down to keep them from moving around during transport from theatre to theatre.

There were drawers full of necklaces, bracelets, earrings, and cuff links. Another drawer full of different eye glasses, and still another with hair clips. I looked in each one, but paid special attention to the drawer of watches. I studied each watch carefully, looking for any sign of a snake, but by the time I finished with the final drawer, I hadn't found anything.

"And this is all of the jewelry?"

She nodded. "That is everything I have."

I sagged with disappointment. The watch was probably logged in police evidence or missing somewhere. The likelihood of finding it now was slim.

"Sorry you didn't find what you needed," she said. "If I knew more, I would love to help. Dressing these actors for as many months as I have, I feel protective of them. It feels like one of my own children was killed that night. If someone is responsible, I'd like to bring them to justice."

"Do you think someone could be responsible for the death?" I asked. "As the costumer, you must have been in contact with every single performer. Did you notice any strains in the relationships?"

She shook her head. "I don't know much about the interpersonal relationships of the actors. I focus on my job and my relationship with each actor. I can only tell you about my experiences."

"And what was your experience like?" I asked.

"With Phineas?" She shrugged. "Good. He was a very committed actor. He took his job seriously and wanted to give the best performance he could. I work in a similar manner, so I understood his intense energy. Not everyone else did."

"What about Alfred Grey?" I asked, making little effort to be subtle. "I spoke with your assistant, Judith, and she seemed very fond of the man. She didn't care for Phineas as much."

"Judith enjoys drama both on the stage and off," the head costumer said with a hint of fondness. Judith was so open and honest that she was evidently difficult to dislike. "I do not involve myself in that, but I will tell you that my opinion of Alfred Grey is probably less favorable than hers."

"Why is that?" I asked.

She leaned forward, looking out into the hallway to be sure we were alone before she began speaking. "I already told you that I spent the day of the accident repairing Phineas St. Clair's costume. Well, that was only necessary because of Alfred Grey."

"How was he involved?"

"I fitted his costume months ago when the tour began. He and Phineas were both responsible for labeling their costumes and storing them away in their proper locations. So, when Alfred came to me and claimed his costume had become too large, I had no reason to believe he was wrong. He was a thin man already, but it was none of my business if he'd lost weight. I took in his costume on a rush order prior to the first show and learned the very next day that it did not fit when Phineas could not wedge himself into his costume."

"It could have been a mistake," I said.

She raised one brow and tilted her head to the side, lips pressed together in disbelief. "Yes, it could have been a mistake. Alfred could have mistakenly placed his costume into the garment bag labeled with Phineas' name inside Phineas' room. That certainly could have happened."

It was obvious by the tone in her voice that she did not believe that was possible at all.

"I did not accuse anyone of anything, though," she said. She shook her head. "I adjusted the costumes as quickly as I could and kept my thoughts to myself. That is how you keep your job in this business. You focus on your own work and don't mind everyone else. So, that is what I've done and what I will do."

"You don't even want to consider why Alfred may have switched the costumes?" I asked. "Even now that Phineas is dead."

"*Especially* now that Phineas St. Clair is dead," she said. "I make the costumes and they pay me well to do it. That is all I need to know."

Had Alfred switched the costumes in a last effort to get himself on stage? If he thought he deserved more stage time, maybe he was willing to cheat his way there. And if he was willing to cheat to make his dreams come true, was he willing to kill?

I did not have the same luxury as the costumer. She was content to worry about her work and forget everything else, but as I walked down the hallway and back across the stage, headed for the lobby of the theatre, thoughts and theories swirled in my mind like water down a drain.

11

Once again, I'd spent the entire morning in the theatre, and the sun was midway across the sky when I stepped outside. I was so busy looking up that I almost didn't notice the man standing at the base of the stairs.

"Excuse me," I said, darting around him to avoid a collision.

"Alice?"

I stopped and looked up to see Thomas standing in front of me. He wore a tan suit with a dark coat over it that hung down to his knees, and a twin of my own surprised expression.

"Thomas," I said, his name coming out like a question. "What are you doing here?"

I glanced up at the clock on the face of the theatre to be sure of the time. "We weren't meant to meet here for another hour."

His mouth opened and closed twice before he finally found the words. "I feel foolish now, but I was afraid of being late. I didn't want you to be here waiting for me any longer than necessary, so—"

"You arrived two hours before the show?" I asked in a teasing voice.

I knew the day before that Thomas was taken with me. He followed me around the theatre and eagerly asked me to go to the show with him. But arriving this early for our engagement seemed eager even by his standards.

"See? I told you I felt foolish," he said with a smile.

A collection of reporters stood behind him, and he pressed a hand to my back and led me further away from them. For the better, too. My family had been out of the news for several years, but there were still plenty of journalists eager to write a line about us if given the chance.

"Please don't feel foolish. Timeliness is a desirable quality in a person," I said. "Better early than late."

"My motto." He smiled and then tilted his head to the side in question. "Why are you here so early?"

"Mr. Williamson required my help," I said truthfully. "I was just leaving to get some food before meeting with you. Have you eaten yet?"

"Yes, but that won't stop me from escorting you," Thomas said, presenting his elbow to me. "Where to?"

We walked to a café two blocks over. Thomas ordered tea, and I took the special, an asparagus soup.

When our waitress left to fulfill our order, Thomas folded his hands in front of him on the table and leaned forward. "You said you were helping Mr. Williamson?"

"He is an old family friend," I said, hoping to dodge the question. "He and my parents have known each other for years. So long I'm not even sure when they first met."

"He must be quite fond of you, as well, to ask you for help." It was just a statement, but I could see the question lurking underneath.

"I'm fond of him, as well," I said. "He is a nervous man, but I suppose running a popular theatre could make anyone nervous. There are a lot of moving parts to contend with."

"The recent tragedy has him even more nervous, I assume." Once again, the question was unspoken but present between us. "Everyone is talking about the death of Phineas St. Clair.

I nodded. "It was a tragedy. Mr. Williamson is dealing with the repercussions of the death as well as trying to continue with the show. I want to help him in any way I can."

"Have you spoken with any of the performers?" Thomas asked. "Was it their decision to continue with the play?"

"It seems to have been a group decision, though I am not privy to the inner workings of that discussion. I've only briefly spoken with a few members of cast. My friendship with Mr. Williamson does not extend to the actors."

Thomas nodded and brushed his golden hair from his forehead. "Sorry if I'm a bit overeager."

"I understand," I said. "You want to be an actor yourself. I'm sure you are interested in how things work behind the scenes. That is why you went on the tour, after all."

The corner of his mouth turned up in a smile but it faded quickly, giving way to thin-lipped determination. "I know you don't know much about the actors, but has Mr.

Williamson told you anything about the ruling the police are leaning towards?"

He had, but I felt strange speaking on the subject. Especially since I did not agree with what the police believed happened. "Mr. Williamson does not want any information leaking out to the public. That is difficult with reporters lurking outside like vultures, but I promised him I would keep any information I learned to myself."

Thomas let out a nervous sounding laugh. "Of course, I understand."

I smiled in apology and then welcomed the distraction of our food and tea arriving. Thomas poured sugar and cream into his tea and stirred it with a small silver spoon. He had a dark smudge on the end of his finger that he must have noticed at the same time I did. He wiped his hand on the napkin and leaned back in his chair.

"I only asked because I have a friend down at the police station." He sipped from his tea, blowing across the surface to cool it down.

"Oh?" I asked, feigning ambivalence.

He nodded. "He told me there was at least one bolt missing from the light, and the coroner found a long thread in Phineas St. Clair's hair. It was brown and frayed on one end, and no one could come up with a good reason why it was there."

I frowned. "A thread?"

"That's what he said. I asked him whether that could point to foul play, and he refused to say anything else. I just wondered whether Mr. Williamson was better informed."

"If he is, he isn't telling me," I lied.

It seemed Mr. Williamson was not well-informed. Or, at least, he was not sharing all of the information he had with me. He'd told me about the bolt that morning, but he hadn't mentioned anything about the thread. Why would he share one piece of information and not the other? The only good explanation I could come up with was that he did not know one piece of information.

Mr. Williamson had told me the police planned to rule the death an accident, but how could they do that if there was evidence they could not explain? Either it was not compelling enough or they did not want to consider the possibility that they had a murder on their hands.

"I suppose we will all know the truth eventually," Thomas said with a sigh.

I swirled a spoonful of soup around in my mouth and nodded. "I suppose we will."

WHEN WE WALKED BACK to the theatre, more people had gathered outside, preparing for that afternoon's matinee performance. Every group we passed was talking about the accident in some way or another.

He died right in the middle of the show. In front of the entire audience.

The understudy is going to take over, but I've never heard of him.

I can't believe they are putting on the show after the lead died.

Was Rosalie Stuart hurt at all?

A horrible accident. Let's hope the rest of the theatre has been inspected.

We weaved our way past the reporters, through the crowds, and into the lobby. The coat check was manned today, so I handed my coat and clutch to a young man in a dark suit and waited as Thomas did the same.

When Thomas turned back to me, arm extended to escort me towards the theatre, he looked over my shoulder and then frowned, his brows creasing. I was about to ask if anything was the matter, but was interrupted.

"I'd forgotten you two planned to come to this performance."

I spun around and was face-to-face with Sherborne Sharp. He took off his hat and reached around me to hand it to the attendant.

"I didn't know you planned to come at all," I said sharply, eyes narrowed. "You didn't mention it yesterday."

"I was in the neighborhood and wanted to see the play the city can't stop talking about." He smiled, but he looked more like a lion looking at its lunch.

"They are only talking about it because of the death," I said. "I doubt half the people here even know what the show is about."

"Make that half plus one," he said. "I must admit I know nothing of the show. I've never been fond of theatre."

"Really? Because you seem like the kind of man who was born to perform."

"You do have a certain presence about you," Thomas agreed naively behind me, not understanding my true meaning.

I could see that Sherborne understood, however. His gaze sharpened before looking away to scan the crowd. "Well, I would not want to interrupt your outing. I don't know anyone else here by first look, but I'm sure I can make friends."

"No need to make friends when you have some at the ready," Thomas said. "Alice and I don't mind if you join us. We won't be talking much once we get into the theatre, anyway."

Sherborne's mouth turned up in a sly smile. "Well, if you two are sure I wouldn't be intruding, then I would love the company."

I wanted to tell Sherborne that I did mind. Not because I was concerned about my time with Thomas being interrupted, but because I knew Sherborne had only come to keep an eye on me. He'd openly admitted he had no interest in theatre. He was only interested in shielding me like an overprotective parent, and I did not need his concern.

I did, however, need his distraction.

Thomas' mention of the thread refused to leave my mind. The costume department had been full of thread, and Phineas had spent the last hours before his death there getting his costume let out. Was it possible the thread could have simply fallen into his hair and remained there throughout the performance? It seemed unlikely considering the action the play required. In just the first act, Phineas had jumped over a prop sofa, danced wildly across the stage with Rosalie, and done a full somersault during a party scene in an effort to entertain his high-society friends. There was no way the thread would have remained in place during all of that.

So, it must have been placed there shortly before his death.

Perhaps, it had somehow been involved in the light falling from the ceiling, though I wasn't sure how.

The thread introduced many questions, but the main one I wanted to answer was this: did a similar thread exist in the costume department? If it did, then someone in the building would have had access to it and could have used it to rig the light to fall at the precise moment they wanted it to. It was a stretch, certainly, but the first step was to get back to the costume department and search the supplies.

"I just remembered that I promised to speak with Mr. Williamson before the show," I said, grabbing Thomas' arm and spinning around, backing away from where he and Sherborne stood in the lobby.

"The show will start soon," he said, glancing at the clock above the doors. "In fifteen minutes."

"I'll be back in time," I assured him, avoiding Sherborne's gaze. Even without looking directly at him, I could tell his eyes were narrowed in suspicion. "Wait here for me, and I'll be back soon."

Before either of them could say anything in argument, I spun away and hurried towards the door marked "employees only."

Cast and crew scurried around the backstage like mice seeking higher ground in a flood. Mr. Williamson's comment that someone could have walked across the stage in their undergarments prior to the show without anyone noticing proved true. Whereas I'd been stopped by several people each time I'd gone behind the curtain before, this time, no one said anything to me.

I walked past dressing rooms where voices carried into the hallway, rehearsing lines and calling for makeup, and into the costume department.

The same nameless woman from before sat in the same chair she'd been in that morning, but now she was working on a different costume.

Without looking up from her work, she knew who I was.

"Come back for something else?" she asked.

"I'd like to look through your collection of threads if you don't mind."

She nodded, not minding my intrusion at all, and I set about looking through the box of thread and bobbins she pointed out.

It didn't take long to find what I was looking for. Every color of the rainbow was represented, but a large majority of the thread in the box—nearly one-third of it —was various shades of brown. Neutral colors to go with most outfits. If someone were to reach into the box randomly, they were more likely to pull out a shade of brown than any other color.

"Find what you needed?" she asked.

"Is this room ever locked?"

She shook her head. "There doesn't seem to be a reason for it. Unless someone wants some bolts of fabric or prop jewelry, there isn't much here to steal."

Anyone could have stopped by here when the room was empty to grab some thread, and she would never notice one missing spool.

Like I thought, the visit didn't answer many questions, but it at least let me know it was a possibility. Someone could have loosened the bolts and tied the light in such a way that it could be released at will. That could explain the frayed end of the thread Thomas had mentioned.

I thanked her for letting me intrude once again and replaced the box in the stack where I'd found it. Then, as I turned to leave, I passed by the shelving I'd examined earlier that morning and noticed a piece of jewelry sitting on top. While the thread spools were just thrown in a box, the jewelry had been strategically organized with each type relegated to its own drawer to make it easy for the costumers to find exactly what they were looking for. So, the gold watch stood out for being out of place. But even more than that, it stood out because of the intricate green design that wrapped around the wristband and across the watch face.

It almost looked like a snake.

I moved towards it slowly, as though it was a real snake that would slither away if I startled it. I almost couldn't believe it. I'd scoured the room earlier, looking through each drawer and examining every item of jewelry. And now, here it was, sitting right on top of the dresser in plain sight.

Phineas' watch.

Or rather, the watch Lady Haddington had gifted to him. It had to be the same one. Gold watches with jeweled snakes inlaid into the design were not exactly common fashion. I had never seen one before, and would likely never see one similar again. It was a one-of-a-kind piece, difficult to miss.

So, how had I missed it before?

I grabbed the watch, rubbing it through my fingers to convince myself it was real. Then, I tucked it into my palm and closed my fingers around it.

"Has anyone else been in here since I left a couple of hours ago?" I asked.

The costumer let out a harsh laugh. "Everyone has been in here. We have a show starting in a few minutes. I had actresses missing wigs and shoes and stockings, and actors in need of mustache wax and belts."

Anyone could have dropped the watch off. If the person responsible for Phineas' death realized the watch was somehow connected, they could have left it in the costume department, hoping it would get lost in the large pile of fake jewelry.

If they'd wanted that to happen, however, they should have hidden it better.

"You had best get back to the theatre before the show starts," she said.

I jumped, surprised by her voice and feeling guilty for taking the watch. Even though I knew it wasn't really stealing to take something that had never belonged to her in the first place, I still didn't want her to know I had it. So, I lifted my empty hand in a parting wave and hurried back through the backstage towards the main theatre.

THE DISCUSSION in the lobby after the show was drastically different than before. Phineas St. Clair's name was only mentioned so far as it was necessary to discuss how well his replacement had done in the performance.

"I had never heard of Alfred Grey before today, which after seeing him, I can't believe," Thomas said. "That was a remarkable performance."

I nodded in resigned agreement. My opinion of

Alfred was colored from when he'd kicked me out of the backstage area and from the costumer's comments about him. But even I had to admit he'd done an excellent job.

"You are the only one here who saw Phineas in his performance," Thomas said. "So, how did Alfred compare?"

"I only saw Phineas in the first act," I reminded him.

"How did the first act compare?" he asked.

I was notably more focused on the performance this time than the first, but that could have been because my senses were heightened, waiting for another light to come crashing to the stage. Even though the play remained unchanged, the tension felt more palpable.

"He did just as well, at least," I said. Thomas seemed disappointed that I hadn't raved, so I conceded. "Perhaps, even better."

He smiled and turned to Sherborne. "What did you think, Mr. Sharp?"

Sherborne casually slid his hands into his pockets and shrugged. "As I said, I have never been a great lover of theatre. I think the art of it all may be lost on me."

"Don't say such a thing to Thomas, Sherborne. He wants to be an actor one day."

Sherborne looked over Thomas with new eyes, one eyebrow arching slightly in surprise. "If that is so, I'm sure he won't let my disinterest color his dreams."

"Indeed," Thomas said, less enthusiastically than before.

For reasons I did not understand, Thomas seemed to want Sherborne's good opinion and friendship, and Sherborne seemed reluctant to give it.

Suddenly, a fourth party joined our awkward group. It was Mr. Williamson, making a clear beeline for me.

"What did you think of the show, Miss Alice?"

"Everything went perfectly."

He smiled and pressed his palms together, looking upwards. "Thank Heaven for that. Seven more shows without anything unexpected, and perhaps I'll be able to move on and put this entire experience behind me."

"Do you think public memory will fade so quickly?" Thomas asked.

Mr. Williamson seemed startled by Thomas, as if he hadn't seen him standing there, and then frowned at his suggestion. "I've learned that if you put on a good enough show, people can be distracted from just about anything."

Thomas seemed ready to argue, but I jumped in to keep him from upsetting Mr. Williamson any further. "If a good show is what you need, I think you've found it. Alfred did wonderfully."

"He did," he said, no lack of relief in his voice. "Would you like to tell him yourself?"

I looked around, confused, expecting to see Alfred mingling with the crowd in the lobby.

"Not now," Mr. Williamson clarified. "But later at a party. It will be at my house for the entire cast and crew and a few select guests. I'd love to have you."

Getting the chance to mix with the cast in a social setting was the exact opening I needed. I wanted to see how they interacted together and see who, if anyone, could have had the motive to kill Phineas St. Clair.

"And I would love to attend," I said. "I readily accept."

Mr. Williamson looked blankly at Thomas and then

Sherborne Sharp. When his eyes met my taller companion, recognition flickered there.

"Mr. Sharp?"

"Hello, Mr. Williamson," Sherborne said, as though the fact that they knew one another was not a revelation. "It is good to see you again."

"Good, indeed," Mr. Williamson said, shaking Sherborne's hand and then clapping his other hand over the top, sandwiching the shake. "You must come to the party tonight, as well. It will be good to catch up when I have more time. As it is, I must get back to running things around here."

We said our goodbyes, and then I turned to Thomas, whose cheeks were flushed with embarrassment.

"I'm sure you would have been invited had the party been less of a personal affair," I said quietly, wishing Sherborne would walk away and give us a moment. Instead, I could feel him lurking over my shoulder.

Thomas tried to smile, but the expression didn't reach his eyes. "No, I completely understand. I hope you two will have a good time. Be sure to tell me all about it."

"Of course, I will. You are the one interested in theatre anyway. It should be you there."

He waved my words away. "As long as you promise to enjoy yourself, I am content to let you go alone."

He tried to remain cheerful as we left the theatre and parted ways, but I saw the flicker of disappointment in his eyes when Sherborne announced that he would see me later.

12

D espite being invited together, I made no effort to meet up with Sherborne Sharp prior to the dinner party. He was my friend, yes, but lately he had felt more like my minder, and I wanted to dissuade him of that belief. Not to mention, it would be easier to gather the information I wished to gather without someone attached to my side.

I was welcomed into the party by a butler and was surprised by the scope of it. Mr. Williamson had made it feel like a quaint affair, but there were twenty people standing in the living room alone, none of whom I recognized.

I wore a shin-length gold beaded dress and a matching gold turban with my brown hair peeking out the bottom, and I seemed to blend in with the actors and other guests enough that no one paid much attention to me. Still, it was easy for me to pick out the important guests amongst the crowd. Not only did I recognize them from the stage, but their general appearance seemed more luxurious. Rosalie Stuart was dressed in a deep green velvet that complimented the olive tone in her skin and made her gold hair shine even brighter. She was the center of everyone's attention, but I couldn't help but notice a dark-haired man in a simple suit standing behind her wherever she went. I thought he could be a guard hired to protect her—no one would blame her after what had befallen her co-star—but then I saw the way she looked at him when the crowd departed for the snack table, and I knew she thought he was someone special, even if no one else did.

Mr. Williamson said hello to me briefly, but then hurried off to instruct the kitchen staff when to bring out various trays of food. Even at his own party, he couldn't stop himself from overseeing the production of the entire affair.

The vastness of the party dashed any hopes I had of seeing how the actors would interact with one another. They were so surrounded by admirers that they hardly had a chance to speak with one another. In fact, after several passes through the house, I hadn't even seen Alfred Grey yet.

"Are you looking for me, Miss Beckingham?"

I jolted, splashing my champagne over the side of my glass and onto the hardwood floor. I glowered at it and then up at Sherborne Sharp. He had changed into a dark blue suit with velvet lapels. He looked like a more important person than anyone else in the room, and I resented him for it.

"I am not," I said. "I'd almost forgotten you were invited at all."

He sighed and leaned against the wall to my right.

"This animosity is growing tiresome. When did our friendship falter? Have I done something wrong?"

I did not want to argue with Sherborne here in front of everyone. There was also the problem that I wasn't entirely sure why his insistence in watching over me bothered me so much. Many women would be pleased that a man who looked like Sherborne Sharp paid them any mind at all. I, apparently, was not one of the many.

"Have you looked into the matter I asked you to?" I asked. Despite the distraction of the death of Phineas St. Clair, The Chess Master had not left my mind. It was the enduring mystery I was intent upon solving.

"Not yet."

"And do you think being at this party will allow you to uncover some information on that subject?" I knew I was being unfair. I couldn't expect Sherborne to spend every spare second on my case. However, I was too frustrated to be rational.

Sherborne clenched his jaw. "It is hard to say where a clue may come from, but no, I do not expect to solve the case tonight."

"Then we have nothing to talk about."

I pushed away from the wall and crossed the room before Sherborne could say anything else, darting between two stage hands as they began performing what was probably a popular party trick to the delight of many onlookers.

Mr. Williamson's house was a series of small, intimate rooms connected by a main hallway. Everything was wood-panelled and grand, highlighting his family's long history of successful business dealings in the city. Had he not informed me of the theatre's financial struggles, I never would have guessed he was in any trouble at all.

I walked down the hallway, past the sitting room, a study, and a dining room with a long table covered in finger foods, cakes, and puddings. I kept walking because I did not want to hesitate and give Sherborne the opportunity to catch up to me.

I kept walking until I found myself outside of a room I had not gone inside yet. It was at the far end of the house from the main party, but the door was opened a sliver, leading me to believe the room was part of the festivities. However, as soon as I pushed the door open a bit more, two distinct voices floated into the hallway, and their tone stopped me in place.

"I should have called off the entire party. I should have cancelled the moment I heard. It took all of my energy to make it through the performance, and now I have nothing left. I can't go out there and pretend everything is all right," said a male voice.

"Everything *is* all right, Joseph," a female voice said.

Finally, I recognized the voice. Joseph. Joseph Williamson.

"You think this is all right?" Mr. Williamson boomed. "My personal guest would rather be on the arm of the young actors I employ. I look like a fool, Cornelia."

I had to cover my mouth to contain my gasp of surprise. Cornelia Haddington was Mr. Williamson's personal guest.

My mind whirred through my conversation with Mr. Williamson that afternoon. I'd told him about the card I'd found in Phineas' room. I'd told him that Lady Haddington spoke of a possible affair with the young actor. At the time, Mr. Williamson had gone pale and stumbled away from our conversation in a daze, and now it all made sense. Mr. Williamson was seeing Lady Haddington and had no idea she was being unfaithful.

"No one knows of my past relationship with Phineas," Lady Haddington said. "You have nothing to feel foolish about."

"You sent him flowers to *my* theatre two days ago. That seems very present to me."

"You read the card?" she asked, her voice quiet. Ashamed.

I worried he would mention my name. I was looking into the case as a favor. I had no intention of becoming an enemy of Lady Haddington, no matter how much my mother would approve. It would give her an excuse to skip all social events where Cornelia Haddington was in attendance, which was all she'd ever wanted.

Thankfully, Mr. Williamson kept my identity anonymous. "It does not matter how I know what I know. The only thing that matters is I know it, and you lied to me. You sent him flowers and a gift. Why would you do that if you weren't trying to win his affection? Why would you do that if your relationship was in the past?"

"It matters to me how you know, considering the letter was private. How many people have read it?"

"It doesn't matter," Mr. Williamson repeated, his voice booming.

"What happened to the gift and the letter after..."

After he died. Lady Haddington couldn't bring herself to say the words. I wondered if she was still suffering from the same emotional distress she'd been suffering from the day she'd had to cancel her benefit event.

"Is that the only reason you are distressed?" Mr. Williamson asked. "Because you want to know what happened to the jeweled snake watch you gifted to your young lover?"

I replayed my conversation with Mr. Williamson in my head, and nowhere in it did I mention the design on the watch. I did not tell him about the snake, and at the time, I didn't even know it was jeweled. So, how did he?

"Is that why you agreed to be my guest at the theatre?" Mr. Williamson continued. "Not because you cared about me, but because you wanted to see Phineas perform? Well, you certainly got a performance."

Lady Haddington gasped. "Joseph, that is a horrible thing to say. The man is dead. You aren't being fair. Our relationship was not confirmed. I did not know I was not allowed to admire the work of a young actor. This party is the first time we have been seen together in public, so you cannot pretend we were devoted to one another."

Mr. Williamson snorted. "We weren't devoted to one another because of your scruples about our relationship. You worried it would make your late husband look bad if you moved on too soon, but I think you forget he already looked bad. Criminal connections don't look good on anyone."

"That is quite enough!" Lady Haddington shouted. The rest of the party was loud enough that I knew she wouldn't be heard by anyone, but still, the argument seemed to be reaching a point where either of them could storm out at any second. I did not want to be caught listening at the door when they did. So, as quietly as I'd come, I retreated back down the hallway to the party.

I moved aimlessly through the crowd as my mind focused on the conversation I'd overheard. Lady Haddington had been in the audience the night of Phineas' death. She hadn't been standing backstage ready to drop a light on Phineas' head. She could have hired someone to do it for her, but at least I knew she had not done it herself, which moved her to the bottom of my suspect list.

Mr. Williamson, surprisingly, had moved up.

How did he know about the jeweled snake? If he was engaged in a romance with Lady Haddington, it was possible he had seen the watch before, but if their relationship was as new as Lady Haddington made it sound, I doubted they were at that level of familiarity.

Also, there was the matter that the watch had been dropped off at the costume department a few hours after I told him about it. Could that be a coincidence? If it wasn't, why would he have put it in the costume department? Why did he have it at all?

I was still asking myself the endless string of questions when the crowd around me erupted in cheers, and I turned to see Alfred Grey strut through the door.

He waved to the crowd like this level of notice was normal. Like he had always been the lead of a successful play rather than the unknown understudy. He seemed quite comfortable in the spotlight that had been meant for his deceased castmate.

The guests surged around him, congratulating him on his performance and begging for behind the scenes details. Alfred was more than willing to accommodate their questions, and he smiled and regaled the party with talk of his pre-show prepara-

tions and how he put himself in the mind of the
character.

"Acting has always felt more natural to me than being
in my own skin," he said. "It seems easier to take on the
personality of someone else than to go on being boring
old me another day."

The crowd assured him he was far from boring, but I
couldn't help but wonder if there wasn't more to his
words than he let on. If Alfred wasn't hiding more of
himself than anyone knew. What if it was all an act?

I stayed on the edge of the party, observing and
watching as Alfred made his way around the room.
Women, both married and single, fawned over him,
much to the chagrin of their male companions.

Alfred was not a strikingly handsome man. Not in the
effortless way Phineas St. Clair had been. Alfred moved
with stiff, rehearsed movements, and he had too much
grease in his hair. He looked like a child stuck in itchy
church clothes rather than a film star in a fabulous suit.

When he finally broke away from his admirers and
found his way to the snack table, he tugged at the collar
of his suit like it was strangling him.

I was standing just to the left of the table, my back
pressed against the wall—in the perfect position to watch
as Judith finally approached Alfred. She pressed her
hands together in front of her simple cotton dress and
looked up at him with a smile.

"I only saw the performance from backstage, but you
were wonderful," she said.

Alfred nodded distractedly and reached for a
cucumber sandwich. "Thank you."

"Really," she insisted. "Tonight was the best performance I can remember seeing from the entire run of the show so far."

"Thank you, Judith," Alfred said, never turning to fully face her.

Judith shifted on her heels, her fingers tangling nervously in front of her. "I know you are busy talking with your admirers, but I hoped we would have a few minutes to talk this evening. Things have been so busy at the theatre that there hasn't really been any time."

Her voice was low, intimate. She leaned forward as she spoke like her words were a secret, but Alfred just bobbed his head. "Yes, of course. I can always make time for my ardent followers."

Judith blinked slowly, and I could see her trying to decide if he was referring to her as a follower or not. Before she could decide, a gaggle of young socialites approached Alfred and drew his attention away. In the middle of the group, he floated back into the sitting room, leaving Judith behind.

She bit down on her lip and was looking at the floor when I approached, eyes going glassy.

"Judith?"

Her eyes snapped up to my face, and she swiped at her cheeks even though she hadn't yet started to cry. "Oh, hello, Miss Beckingham. I didn't know you'd be here."

"Mr. Williamson just invited me after the show," I said. "How are you enjoying the party?"

Her pale skin revealed her every emotion. Her cheeks were stained red with anger or embarrassment or a mixture of both. "It's fine."

I nodded, wanting to protect her dignity, but also hoping to comfort her in some way if I could.

"Alfred is quite popular tonight. I'm sure he is just distracted by—"

"Mr. Grey is none of my business," she snapped, grabbing a small sandwich from the platter.

I leaned in, voice low. "I'm sorry if I suggested anything. You just seemed upset and—"

"I'm not upset," she interrupted. Then, she lifted a hand in an impatient wave. "I'm going to make my way around the party. Goodbye, Miss Beckingham."

After trying and failing to make Judith feel better, I was hesitant to talk with anyone else at the party. Truly, I wasn't in the mood for a party. With questions about the watch, Lady Haddington, and Mr. Williamson floating around my mind, I was distracted. So distracted I didn't realize I was standing next to Alfred Grey until I noticed a few women across the room staring at me with obvious annoyance in their eyes. I couldn't understand why they'd dislike me without meeting me until I noticed their gazes flicking to the man to my right.

"Mr. Grey." I said his name mostly out of surprise, but then he turned to me, face blank and confused. When he saw me, however, he smiled.

"I'm sorry. I don't think we've been introduced yet."

The night he'd seen me on the theatre stage, Alfred's expression had been one of thinly-veiled disgust. Tonight, he looked at me with interest, apparently not recognizing me from before. His eyes perused my beaded dress and then trailed back up to my face, skimming the surface of me as if trying to see if I was worth his time. Apparently, I was.

"Alice Beckingham," I said, holding out a hand.

Alfred grabbed it eagerly, pulling my knuckles to his

mouth. His hands were dry and cold, but his breath was warm on the back of my hand. Goosebumps rolled down my back and across my shoulders.

"You already know my name," he said. "It is a strange thing—being famous. People know you before you've even met."

Alfred said it was strange, but he seemed to find it all quite exhilarating. I'd never seen someone take to a way of life faster than he had. He was born to be in the spotlight.

"Actually, I knew your name prior to your role in the play," I admitted. "I am a friend of Mr. Williamson. I've seen you around the theatre."

He nodded and leaned forward. "Then why haven't I seen you?"

I leaned away from him on instinct. I could not pretend to be interested in a man I cared nothing for, not even if it meant gathering much needed information.

"I do not crave the spotlight the way others do. That is why I am not an actress."

"You could be," he said quickly. "At least, you have the looks for it. People want to look at beautiful people on stage."

In his compliment to me, he had also complimented himself. Except, Alfred Grey did not strike me as better looking than the average man. Sherborne Sharp had a more appealing face than Alfred.

"That is true," I agreed. "Phineas St. Clair was a beautiful person."

Alfred's nose wrinkled. "Indeed."

"It is horrible what happened to him," I said.

"Truly tragic," he said with a sigh. "Forgive me, but

I'm quite tired of discussing the matter. It is not really party conversation and it upsets me to remember it all."

"Were you there the night it happened?"

"The entire cast was. I stood just off stage."

"I was in the audience, too," I said. "I came with my parents. My poor mother was distraught by the sight, though not as distraught as you were, I'm sure. It must have been devastating. Then again, maybe not."

Alfred frowned. "Maybe not? Why would you say that?"

I tipped my head to the side and shrugged. "I don't like to give credence to rumors, but I've heard whispers that you and Phineas St. Clair were not the closest of friends. Not to say his death wouldn't be sad, but perhaps you are not as devastated as some others."

"Whispers from who?" he asked, eyes narrowed.

"Just conversation around the theatre," I said as casually as I could. "People thought there might be tension between the two of you over stage time. I didn't ask for details."

"You should have," he snapped. "That is ridiculous. Phineas and I worked together for months. If we'd had any difficulties working together, everyone would have known."

"I'm not so certain they would have," I said. "The relationship between a lead and his understudy is rarely important news."

Alfred's nostrils flared at the suggestion he was not important news, and I hoped I wasn't pushing him too far. I just wanted him to be uncomfortable enough to let something slip. To say something he wouldn't normally say and let me in on the relationship between him and

Phineas St. Clair. People rarely let details slip when they were comfortable. I needed to ruffle his delicate feathers.

"You've claimed not to give much credence to gossip, but I'd suggest you give none at all. These accusations are unfounded and untrue. Phineas and I were good friends, and I am just as devastated by his loss as anyone else, perhaps even more so. Any suggestion to the contrary is hurtful."

"I was not making any accusations," I said, lifting my hands in defense. "I'm sorry if I suggested otherwise. If you and Phineas were good friends, then I'm sure it was apparent to everyone and they already know that."

"I do not often let anyone in on my private life," he said. "It does not matter to me what anyone else knows or does not know about my personal life and the connections therein. The only thing that matters to me is that I know I was friends with Phineas St. Clair."

I said, "Few people are self-confident enough to care nothing for the opinions of others, so congratulations."

Alfred Grey stepped away from me and frowned, his fuzzy brows furrowed. Rather than taking in the entirety of my frame, he focused on my face this time, narrowing his attention. I saw recognition flicker across his face.

"We have met before."

My heart lurched in my chest. "We have?"

"You were there," he said. "The night of the accident. On the stage."

He remembered. I'd pegged Alfred Grey as a man too self-important to notice or care about a nameless bystander. Yet, he remembered me.

"You came backstage to see his body the night of his

death. I had you removed." He shook his head and took another step away. "How did you get into this party?"

"I'm friends with Mr. Williamson," I said, my voice shaky. It was true. Alfred could challenge it, and I knew Mr. Williamson would defend my right to be here. Yet, I still felt like I'd been caught. "He invited me to the party. It is the reason I was backstage that night, as well."

That was a lie, but Alfred didn't know.

"Mr. Williamson has many friends," he said. "But you are the only friend of his who has shown such an interest in the death of an actor you did not know. If I didn't know better, I'd think you were hiding something."

I shook my head, words lodged in my throat like a stone. I couldn't seem to speak or find anything to say. I just stood in front of him and shook my head.

Finally, Alfred lifted one eyebrow, glanced around the room to be sure no one was listening in, and then leaned forward to deliver his parting line.

"You should be careful, Miss Beckingham. As interested as you are in this matter, someone is liable to think you were involved in Phineas' death. And I'd hate to see you get hurt."

His mouth turned up in a smile for just a second before he stood tall, turned on his heel, and moved into the crowd, opening his arms wide to the women desperate to be close to him. I stayed in the same place, my back pressed against the wall, and took deep breaths to keep from falling down.

13

I was so shaken from my conversation with Alfred Grey that I didn't even attempt to run away when Sherborne Sharp walked into the room and cut straight towards me. He leaned against the wall at my left and bent down to speak in my ear.

"Are you all right? You look pale."

"Have you always been such a charmer?" I asked. "With compliments like that, it is a miracle you are still unmarried."

He sighed. "You are deflecting. Whatever has happened, you might as well just tell me. I'll find it out eventually."

I rolled my eyes. "You do not have time to find it out. At least you shouldn't. Not when I've given you a job to do."

"Alice," Sherborne said, his voice pleading. "I'm sorry if I've upset you. I promise you it was unintentional. But I can't handle your animosity anymore."

"And I cannot handle your doting anymore." I

clenched my hands into fists and pushed away from the wall. I felt unsteady, as though the ground was shifting under my feet, and I realized it was probably more about the two glasses of champagne I'd had on an empty stomach than anything Alfred Grey had done or said.

"My doting?" Sherborne asked, his tan face wrinkled in confusion.

I gestured with both hands to his presence in front of me. "You have searched the entire party to find me and see if I am all right when you should not even be here in the first place. I do not need you checking up on me or worrying for me. I did not ask you to come."

"Mr. Williamson did," he said. "I did not want to reject his invitation and risk seeming rude."

"Since when have you cared about being rude?"

"I care more than you do, apparently," he said, raising his voice for the first time.

The flare of passion in his eyes surprised me. Sherborne always maintained his composure. He kept calm in the face of danger and remained level-headed in all matters. The fact that I had pushed him to anger was startling.

"I had it in my mind that we were friends," Sherborne said sourly. "I believed that you had come to appreciate my presence as more than just your errand boy, but clearly, I was wrong. You want me to be like your dog, fetching what I am told to fetch and nothing else. If that is what you want, fine. I will not concern myself in your personal matters beyond what you allow me to know. But you do not get to keep me from engaging with society. If we run into one another at an event, I will not be made to feel like a lovesick puppy who follows you around. I will not be made to look like a fool for you, Alice."

Frustration stung the backs of my eyes, tears prickling the corners, but I stiffened my upper lip and glared at him, pushing back the emotion. "That is all I've wanted from you. I need information and nothing more."

Hurt flashed across his face for only a second before he composed himself. Sherborne stood to his full height, his shoulders broad and confident, and looked away from me. His square jaw clenched, and then he dipped his head low, arm pressed to his stomach in a bow.

"Good evening, Miss Beckingham. I've had enough socializing for the evening."

Before I could say anything, he strode off through the party and out of the room.

I DIDN'T STAY at the party much longer after Sherborne left. Every conversation I'd had all evening had ended in anger and confusion, and I was tired of fighting. My mind felt muddled by the time I made it home, and I wanted to go straight to my room and to bed. Unfortunately, my mother was waiting for me in the sitting room.

"You are home early," she called.

I moved into the entryway and leaned against the door. "I'm tired. I wasn't in a party mood."

She frowned. "Mr. Williamson usually knows how to throw a rousing affair. I'm surprised it didn't liven you up."

I didn't want to lengthen the conversation, but I also

couldn't pass up the seamless transition that had been offered.

"Mr. Williamson may have been distracted from his party duties by his lady companion. Did you know he was seeing Lady Haddington?"

My mother had been sitting in the chair with a book in her lap, but suddenly, she stood up and the book skittered across the floor and partially under the couch. Her mouth fell open and her eyes went wide. "You cannot be serious."

"I am," I said. "She co-hosted the event with him, and I saw them talking privately in a room. It looked rather intimate."

She shook her head. "Perhaps it was a benefit of some kind? They could have decided to join their forces in order to raise additional money. Is that possible?"

"It is possible," I admitted with an uncertain shrug. "Though, it seems unlikely. He all but said they were romantically connected."

I could relay the entire conversation I'd overheard, but that would identify me as an eavesdropper, and I did not want my mother to think I was still the same young girl who would press my ear to any closed door.

Mama shook her head again and then sat back down, her shoulders sagging. "I am shocked, but not surprised, if that makes sense."

"It does not." I laughed.

"I'm shocked at the coupling of their personalities, but not that they would each be in want of company," she said. "Mr. Williamson was a source of solace for Lady Haddington after her husband died. He offered her seats to the theatre and invited her to all of his parties. He told me once he was worried about her being lonely, and I thought it was very kind of him to care about her. I, of course, never expected he would be interested in her since he had never shown an interest in any woman. Mr. Williamson's first and only love had always been his theatre. He had time for little else."

"Apparently, he made time."

"Apparently." She nodded in agreement and then frowned; her nose wrinkled. "I always hoped that when Mr. Williamson finally settled down, it would be with a more respectable woman. A true partner for him. He is such a kind man."

In all of my interactions with Mr. Williamson over the years, he had always struck me as a true businessman through and through. He was concerned about what he could get out of an interaction. That did not necessarily make him a bad man, but it meant that he rarely kept company that did not benefit him in some way. When Edward was in the news for his crimes and death, we heard less often from Mr. Williamson. That was the case with many of my parents' friends, but he was amongst them. That alone kept me from calling him a kind man. Mr. Williamson, rather, was a calculating man.

What did a relationship with Lady Haddington gain him?

"I am happy he is happy," my mother said, not at all convincingly. "He deserves to be with someone even if it is not the person I would choose for him to be with."

Again, was he happy? My mother based her feelings on the idea that Mr. Williamson was kind and deserving of happiness, but was he either of those things?

I went up to my room with the excuse that I was tired —which was true—but sleep eluded me.

The snake watch did not appear in the costume department until after I'd told Mr. Williamson it was a key piece of evidence. Also, I had not mentioned the appearance of the watch to him at all, yet he had described it perfectly to Lady Haddington.

Could Mr. Williamson have stolen the watch from Phineas St. Clair's dressing room? And if so, why?

I knew better than to jump to conclusions. He could have simply mentioned the missing watch to someone in the theatre and, in places like that, word would travel quickly. It could have reached the killer and led them to discard the evidence in a place they hoped no one would notice it.

Or, Mr. Williamson could have done it.

No matter how I tried to excuse him, my thoughts went back to the very man who had asked me to investigate the death in the first place.

Very little made sense to me in that moment, but I knew one thing for certain: I would need to be more careful with the information I shared with Mr. Williamson throughout the rest of the investigation. No one could be trusted.

14

I saw the headline in the paper before I could even sit down for breakfast. Printed in large black ink on the front of my father's paper were these words: *Actor's Death Ruled Accident.*

"Alice," my father chastised when I grabbed the paper out of his hands and separated the front page from the rest. I handed it back to him, and he glared in my direction for a second before going back to his reading. I barely noticed.

Actor's Death Ruled Accident

After a thorough investigation, the public death of Phineas St. Clair at *The Royal Coliseum* Friday last has been ruled accidental. An improperly hung light fell to the stage below and crushed the actor, killing him almost immediately. Medical professionals in the audience rushed to his aid, but there was little that could be done.

"I never in my life thought I'd live to see such a thing," one audience member said. "It was a ghastly sight. I was three rows back, and I will never erase the image from my mind."

"Phineas would want us to continue the show," the understudy Alfred Grey said the night of the accident. "I don't know what the theatre will decide, but I am pushing for our stop here in London to be seen through until the end. It is what Phineas would have wanted." Several other actors said the same of Phineas St. Clair, and the owner of the theatre, Joseph Williamson, respected the wishes of the actors and allowed the performances to continue. One must ask, however, whether this decision benefitted the actors or the theatre more? If the actors had refused to perform, Mr. Williamson would have lost a great deal of money. Now that the death has been ruled accidental, he may lose a great deal of money, regardless. I, for one, would not want to perform on the same stage where Phineas St. Clair died. "More than death, one must be worried about thievery," an anonymous theatre-goer said. "I and many others I know have left the theatre with less jewelry than when we entered. Purses have been stolen, watches and bracelets snatched from wrists, and even pearl necklaces." When asked about the thefts, Mr. Williamson had only this to say: "The police should be more concerned about the murder of Phineas St. Clair than petty theft. His death was no accident." The police disagree and denied Mr. Williamson's claims that the death was an inside job. With one mystery solved, the only one that remains is whether *The Royal Coliseum* will be able to withstand such a scandal. This is surely the largest that has rocked the theatre since its inception, and we are all waiting with bated breath to see whether this London landmark will remain standing or whether, like the light that killed Mr. St. Clair, it will all come crashing down.

"I would not bother reading that," my father said when I was halfway through the article. "It paints a poor picture of our friend. I can't believe the paper would publish it. It is more of an opinion piece than anything informative."

When I finished the article, I folded it in half and laid my hands over the top, trying to absorb what I'd just read.

"Poor Mr. Williamson," my father said, shaking his head.

My father was not one to pity others or to be overly concerned with their emotional wellbeing. The fact that even he felt for Mr. Williamson meant this article was precisely as bad for *The Royal Coliseum* as I imagined.

As quickly as possible, I ate breakfast and headed to the theatre.

Mr. Williamson was pacing in his office when I arrived. His receptionist, a wide-eyed young woman with shaking hands, stood silently in the corner, nodding as he raved on.

"The article is lies," he said, shaking the paper in the air. "I never spoke with a single newspaper reporter. I tried actively to keep them out of the theatre altogether. The quote is a lie!"

"But," the receptionist said, pausing to gather her strength, "don't you believe his death was a murder?"

"Of course, I do," he said. "But I did not say that to the press."

"Perhaps someone overheard you speaking in the lobby," I said, announcing my presence.

Mr. Williamson spun around and narrowed his eyes. "You did not have anything to do with this article, did you?"

I shook my head. "I haven't spoken to any reporters. You know how my family feels about them."

He took a breath and then nodded, his anger slipping into sympathy for a second. "I nearly forgot. Of course."

I closed his office door behind me. "I came as soon as I read the article."

"The article," he growled. "The police did not warn me they were releasing the findings of the investigation. I thought I would have time to prepare for such an announcement. Truly, I hoped you would find the truth before this happened. Now that it has been announced, I can't change people's minds."

"Yes, you can," I argued. "If we solve this case and announce the truth, people will believe it."

"Some will. But some will always think it was an accident. A cover-up to protect my name." He sighed and sunk down into his leather chair. "The article also mentions reports of thievery. No one will want to come to a theatre where they will be robbed and then crushed by falling debris."

I glanced at the receptionist, hoping she could be of some help, but she was just standing against the wall with her eyes glued to the floor. I brushed past her and sat in the chair opposite Mr. Williamson's desk.

"Things seem bad now, but I know I am getting close to solving the case."

He looked up, forehead wrinkled. "You are?"

I nodded, hoping I looked convincing. "Once I do, everything will be right again. I promise."

Mr. Williamson ran a hand down his face, pulling his bottom lip down, and closed his eyes. "I'm not sure I should ask you to waste your time any longer, Alice. You have been very supportive these last few days, but I need to focus on my public image. I need to do what I can to let people know they can trust me and their time spent inside *The Royal Coliseum*. This investigation is becoming a distraction I can't afford."

"No, you can't give up yet," I said more loudly than I intended.

"I am not giving up," he said. "I simply know when I am wasting my time."

"This is not a waste of time."

"I'm sorry I got you involved, Alice," Mr. Williamson said.

"I was involved even before you asked. I agree with you. Phineas St. Clair's death was no accident. Your permission to be here advanced my investigation in ways I can't explain, but I was investigating his death even before you asked. We cannot give up on finding justice so quickly."

Mr. Williamson tipped his head to the side. "Between

the death and the charges of theft, I have too much to deal with. Acts are going to begin cancelling, and if I want to save my theatre, I have to convince them they have nothing to worry about."

"You do that, then, and let me worry about the case," I said. "You will not even know I am here."

I could tell Mr. Williamson was not sold on the idea. He wanted to be done with the investigation, and if he revoked my access to the theatre, solving the crime would be much more difficult.

I wanted to share with him my theories. That the death could have been motivated by jealousy on the part of the understudy or one of Phineas's girlfriends or that the robberies—including that of my mother's bracelet the night of Phineas' death—and the murder could have been connected. Perhaps, Phineas realized someone stole the snake watch from him, and he was killed before he could tell who had stolen it. His death could have been a robbery gone wrong. But I could not share any of that with Mr. Williamson because, as I'd learned the day before, I could not trust that he himself was not involved in some capacity.

"One more day," I said, afraid he would refuse me entirely. "Just one more day and then I will drop the matter entirely and do as you wish."

"Do you really think one more day could make the difference?" he asked, one eyebrow raised.

"Every day counts."

He sighed, twisted his mouth to one side, and then nodded. "Fine. One more day."

I smiled and was prepared to thank him when there

was a knock on his office door. He called for the person to
come inside, and Alfred Grey stepped through the door.

He did not look startled to see me there.

"Hello, Miss Beckingham," he said, nodding to me. I
was surprised he remembered my name after our brief
interaction from the party.

He quickly turned his attention to Mr. Williamson. "I
read the article this morning as many people have, and I
want to assure you that no one in the theatre company is
concerned about any further accidents."

"They shouldn't be as it was not an accident," Mr.
Williamson growled.

Alfred nodded. "Either way, we are happy to continue
working with you and in the theatre, and I hope that can
be of some comfort to you right now."

"Thank you, Alfred," Mr. Williamson said. "That is
nice to know. I hope all future actors who walk through
my doors feel similarly. I want everyone to feel welcome
here."

"I have felt welcome and have not noticed anything
stolen from me, despite expensive pieces lying about my
dressing room."

Mr. Williamson's mouth tightened into a tense smile.
"I'm relieved."

"Anyway," Alfred said with a final nod. "I know you
are busy, so I will excuse myself."

"Thank you for your kindness," Mr. Williamson said
as Alfred turned to leave.

However, it was not kindness I saw radiating off of
Alfred Grey as he turned towards the door and leveled a
glare at me. Apparently, he was still annoyed over my

rebuff the night before. Or, perhaps, his anger flowed from another source I did not understand.

Regardless, I had one more day to answer all of the questions that floated around in my mind, so soon after Mr. Grey left, I followed him out and set to work.

15

W hen I knocked on Rosalie Stuart's dressing
room door, I did not know whether she
would be inside or not. It was just as likely
she would be at the hotel next door since it was so early
in the day. However, she opened her door at once.

"Hello," she said, faint recognition crossing her face.
"I'm sorry, I've forgotten your name."

"Alice Beckingham," I said, extending my hand in
greeting.

She took it, and we shook.

"When we met, I was still shaken from the death of
my co-star," she said. "I was not in a place to be making
new friends."

"And how are you feeling now? I know the pain is still
fresh, but I hope you are doing all right."

She turned and grabbed the newspaper I'd seen too
many times already that day and pointed to the headline.
"I thought this might bring me some level of comfort, but
it doesn't. Now that I know it was an accident, I can't help

but think how easily the light could have fallen on me instead."

"But it didn't." Simple words, but true nonetheless. There was no point dwelling on what hadn't happened.

Rosalie shrugged and then folded the paper, tucking it under her arm. "I assume this isn't about your investigation, considering the police have closed the case."

"It is, actually," I admitted. "The police have an idea about what happened here, but I have another. I hope that is not difficult for you to hear."

"Not at all," she said. "Forgive me, but I tend to trust in the opinion of the police. Though, I am interested in what you have to say."

"Forgiven." I smiled. "In your position, I would feel the same way. Do you mind if I come in and speak with you, anyway?"

Rosalie stepped aside and pulled the door open. "Please. Come in."

Her dressing room was bare except for the same sort of furniture I'd seen in Phineas' room Saturday morning and a gold case of makeup sitting on the vanity. Her script pages were stacked neatly on the coffee table next to a cup of still steaming tea.

She gestured for me to sit in the armchair in the corner, and she sat on the sofa near me. Rosalie Stuart moved with grace in everything she did. She had on a silk dressing robe and white slippers, yet she looked effortlessly gorgeous. Truly, a woman made to be seen and admired. I felt young and clumsy in comparison.

"I think I've already made my opinion on the matter clear, but I don't want there to be any confusion," I said. "I believe Phineas may have been murdered."

Rosalie inhaled through her nose, as if the mere suggestion of murder increased her anxiety, but then she released the breath and nodded. "Yes, I gathered that."

"Do you have any idea who may have wanted Phineas gone?" I had avoided asking such blatant questions of anyone else since I had no idea who could have been behind the murder, but Rosalie was one of the only people in the entire theatre whose name had not come up in my investigation. By all accounts, she went about her work and left all else alone. She had no role in the drama that played out behind the scenes.

Rosalie raised her brows as she thought, and then quickly shook her head. "I haven't the slightest idea."

"No one comes to mind?" I pressed. "Saying a name is not an accusation. It could just be that you overheard someone arguing with Phineas or saying something cruel about him. Even if you have no reason to believe they murdered him, if you know of anyone who disliked him, that would be very helpful to my investigation. A staff member or co-star. Perhaps, Alfred Grey?"

"Alfred?" Rosalie asked. She shook her head. "No, Alfred and Phineas were rather close, actually."

"They were friends?"

"Well, maybe not friends," she said. "But they worked well together. Alfred ran lines with Phineas often, and they helped one another with their performances. Alfred often stood just off stage throughout our performances, ready to offer encouragement to Phineas between scenes. The same was true of the night Phineas died. Honestly, I'd say Phineas liked Alfred less than Alfred liked Phineas. Despite being the lead in the play, Phineas was insecure. He worried about being replaced or overshadowed. He never said explicitly, but I knew it had to do with money. He could not afford to give away any extra performances to his understudy and lose the pay for them, so the pressure made him a bit temperamental."

"Alfred helped Phineas with his performance?"

She nodded. "Alfred even made a few key changes in the script from time to time. Honestly, he was too talented to be working as an understudy. I think Phineas may have felt threatened by him."

"Did Alfred ever say that he thought he should be the star?"

"No, he would never," Rosalie said. "Though, it was whispered by others in the cast. And spoken openly by some."

"Who?" I asked, thinking I already knew who she meant.

"The costumer's assistant. Judith." Rosalie sighed and rolled her eyes. "She does good work with the costumes, but she is a silly girl. Her feelings for Alfred were apparent to everyone, and she made it no secret that she preferred Alfred's performance as Richard over Phineas'." Rosalie tipped her head to the side and quirked her mouth up like she'd just thought of something. "I guess that is the answer to your original question. You wanted to know if anyone didn't like Phineas, and Judith would certainly fit that description."

I remembered back to my early discussions with Judith and realized she had been open in her disapproval of Phineas. When she thought I was one of his many girlfriends, she told me I would be better off now that he was dead. Those were harsh words, but she'd spoken them with such apparent concern for me that I hadn't realized exactly how callous they were. Judith really did not like Phineas.

"Yes," Rosalie said, shaking her head in disbelief that she hadn't thought of it sooner. "Judith spoke ill of Phineas to anyone who would listen. It was very unprofessional. Also, I have it on good authority that Judith is the reason Phineas' costume was tailored to Alfred's specifications on Friday night."

"You think Judith tricked the costumer into making the change?"

She nodded. "That is what I've heard at least, and I wouldn't be surprised at all to find out it was true."

The costumer had guessed that Alfred was responsible, but she also made an effort not to engage in the theatre drama, so perhaps she was mistaken.

"Why do you think she would do that?" I asked.

Rosalie shrugged. "I couldn't begin to guess why anyone would be so manipulative. Though, if I had to say, it would be because of her fondness for Alfred."

"As an actor?"

"Yes...and as a man. Judith was open about the fact that she appreciated Alfred's physical appearance as well as his talent." Rosalie sighed and then sat upright, eyes wide. "None of this is to say I believe Judith could be a murderer."

"Of course not," I said.

"I am just answering the question honestly. I would never accuse someone of such a thing." Rosalie cleared her throat. "As I said, I trust the official explanation that the death is an accident if the police say so."

"I am not accusing Judith of anything, either," I said.

"This is all just good information to have moving forward with the case."

I could tell Rosalie was not especially comforted by this assurance. There was a deep frown line across her forehead as she grabbed her mug from the table and took a sip. Finally, she turned to me, brows lowered. "Do not tell anyone I told you any of this. No one outside of the cast knows yet, but this is my last week with the company for this performance."

"You are leaving the cast?" I asked, surprised. "Why?"

"I am going to stay here in London," she said, holding out her right hand and sliding a diamond ring from her finger. Then, she smiled as she slipped it onto the ring finger of her left hand. "I'm recently engaged and plan to be married next week."

"Oh, my." I was stunned, not only because I hadn't heard a single whisper of this news in all of the time I'd spent in the theatre, but also because famous actresses rarely stepped out of the spotlight to settle down. I thought that the man who could make Rosalie Stuart do that must be extraordinary. "Congratulations. Who is the lucky man?"

"You wouldn't know him," Rosalie said, smiling to herself as she admired the ring. "He is a lawyer here in the city. I met him last year, and we've been corresponding throughout the duration of the tour."

Rosalie seemed to come out of her daydream all at once, shaking her head and looking at me with seriousness in her eyes. "I just do not want any gossip to detract from my special day. I have done my utmost to make this tour a wonderful one since it will likely be my last tour for a good long while. Phineas' death has already been a dark cloud, and I wouldn't want to find myself in a feud with anyone in the cast or crew."

"I understand," I said, though I didn't at all. How could a simple lawyer from London snag the attention of Rosalie Stuart? Based on her expression, she was very much in love with the man. "No one will know you've spoken with me."

Rosalie nodded in gratitude and then there was a knock on her door. She called for the person to enter, and Judith stepped inside.

The air seemed to thicken with tension, and I wondered if Judith could sense it—that we'd just been speaking about her.

Based on her easy smile, however, she seemed oblivious.

"You are needed in costuming," Judith said to Rosalie. Then, she nodded to me. "Hello again, Miss Beckingham."

I said my goodbyes to both women and parted ways with them in the hallway. Judith led Rosalie to the costume department, and I walked back towards the stage, thinking over the new information I'd acquired.

When I got to the stage, there was a group of men I didn't recognize working there. They didn't have on the black uniforms of the normal stage crew. Rather, they were in pale jumpsuits with a company name I couldn't read embroidered on the pockets.

One of the men, a middle-aged man with a thick mustache, shimmied a metal crowbar into the stage floor and then stomped on the handle with his heavy boots to pry the wood floor up.

I realized they were repairing the spot where the light dented the floor. Where Phineas St. Clair had died.

Several boards had already been pried up and piled inside a garbage bin, ready to be hauled away. I was about to walk past the working men without any hesitation when something stopped me cold.

The man with the mustache tossed the dented board into the garbage bin as I neared it, and as he did, the light caught the board in a new way, and I saw a spot of red.

Blood, I thought before I could stop myself thinking of it.

I'd been surprised the day after Phineas' death that there were no blood stains on the stage. The crew had done a thorough job cleaning up the scene. Or maybe not.

Then, I realized, dried blood would be brown by this point. Not vibrant red.

Curiosity got the better of me, and I rushed forward and reached for the board in the garbage bin.

A hand waved out in front of me, cutting me off. "I'm sorry, Miss. Those boards are full of nails and splintered wood. You'd better be careful."

I brushed past the man, intent on getting to the board despite his protests, and plucked it from the bin.

"No one is supposed to touch any of this," another younger man said to his partner. "Direct orders from the owner to throw these away immediately. He didn't want the press getting their hands on any of it."

The older man sighed and stepped back, shaking his head. "I tried."

I didn't care if they thought I was a crazed admirer or

one of Phineas' girlfriends. I twisted the board and held it up to the light.

The dent in the wood was a violent gash that nearly went all the way through the board. I didn't need to imagine what that same gash would look like in a person. I'd seen enough of Phineas St. Clair after the accident to know.

I angled the board and there it was again, a flash of red. Only this time, I could see that it was not blood, but pencil markings. A red 'X.'

"Did you do this?" I asked, pointing to the 'X.'

"Yeah, we just pulled it out of the floor," the younger man said. "You watched us."

"No, I mean the mark," I said, holding the board closer. "Did you write on it?"

He squinted at the writing, and his partner leaned in closer, too. Then, he shook his head. "No. That wasn't us. I didn't even see it."

"How did you know which boards to pull up? Did anyone mark them for you?" I asked.

The man with the mustache pointed to the gouge. "We were told to pull up every board that looked like this. So, we did. The light falling did the marking for us. Any board with a dent got pried out."

I blinked down at the red 'X' and wondered who would have done it. Why would someone mark this specific board? And with a red pencil?

As soon as the thought crossed my mind, I realized where I'd seen similar markings before. In the costume department.

Dots along dress patterns and scribbled sizes on scrap

paper—red pencil. The costumer had a full cup of them on her desk.

Why would there be an 'X' in the exact spot where Phineas St. Clair died? Because it was not an accident. Someone planned it. Someone with access to red pencils and, if Thomas was right, brown thread.

Someone who hated Phineas St. Clair and believed his understudy was more deserving of the lead role.

The workers had finished their work and dragged their garbage bin full of wood off stage, leaving me behind clutching the dented wood in my white knuckles, struggling to admit the truth to myself.

Judith killed Phineas St. Clair.

I took a deep breath and shook my head. That was a wild accusation. One I had little proof of aside from a red pencil mark and gossip. I needed more proof; something that could convince the police to reopen the investigation and look into Judith as a suspect. The thread would be a good start.

I spun around and looked up at the ceiling. The missing light still had not been replaced, which meant there might still be evidence of tampering there. Perhaps a bit of brown thread left behind. Thomas had said the piece found in Phineas' hair was frayed on one end. Was that because it had been torn in half and a second scrap would be tied to the metal rigging?

Either way, I planned to find out.

I set the wooden floorboard along the edge of the stage and fumbled along the wall for a light switch. The dark curtains sectioned the backstage area into a series of small, dark rooms, and it was enough to make me dizzy.

I moved through the curtained maze slowly, squinting

into the darkness to find a light. Without it, I wouldn't be able to see anything once I was on the bridge that spanned stage left from stage right.

Finally, while pulling aside a curtain, I heard something clatter to the floor and roll towards my feet. It was a flashlight, probably hidden amongst the curtains by a member of the crew to be used during performances. I picked it up and twisted it on. A beam of light shot out, but the dark curtains seemed to absorb the light. Still, it would be enough to make my way up the ladder to investigate the metal rigging above.

I tucked the flashlight under my right arm and began the steep climb up the stairs. With only one hand on the railing, I felt unsteady, but I knew that was mostly my fear talking. I just had to focus on one step at a time, and I would be fine.

I refused to look down, lest I lose my balance and fall. I was about halfway up the staircase when suddenly, something cool wrapped around my ankle. I didn't realize it was a hand until my foot was pulled from the step, and I was falling.

The flashlight fell out from under my arm, and my entire body splayed outwards, trying desperately to grab onto the railing or the staircase. My hands found only air, and I screamed. It was a quick descent, but the seconds turned to hours.

Questions of who was doing this and why mixed in with the intense fear of what would happen when my body hit the wood floor.

Phineas St. Clair had been crushed by a light falling from the ceiling. Was it possible for a human to be crushed from falling half that height? I didn't think so, but the answer to that question also depended on what—or who—was waiting for me on the ground.

My contact with the ground was not clean. My limbs bounced off the stairs, and I flopped onto my back, my head cracking against the wood floor.

Bright spots filled my vision, and I blinked, trying to figure out without moving how badly I was hurt. Then, one of the spots in my vision separated from the others. It became larger, more vibrant.

I squinted up and tried to lift my arm to shield my eyes, but it hurt too badly. Someone was groaning and distracting me. I realized with a sickening twist in my stomach that it was me.

Suddenly, a shadow rose up behind the light. It peeled away from the darkness around me and moved towards me in perfect oblivion, blotted out by the bright light shining in my face.

"Who are you?" I asked, the words dry and broken from my lips.

The bright spot jerked upwards and came back down quickly. There was a painful blow to my head. And everything went black.

16

———

When I woke up, I was home.

For a moment, I wondered whether the entire thing hadn't been a horrible nightmare. A dark imagining of my brain brought on by continued anxiety. That possibility disappeared as soon as I tried to sit up.

The room around me spun, my stomach lurched, and I was forced back into my pillows by my own body and a firm hand against my chest.

"Don't worry, Alice. You're all right."

I turned and saw my mother sitting next to my bed. She was in her nightgown with her hair pinned up on top of her head. She'd been reading in the chair next to my bed, but now she was hovering next to me, her eyes wide and red-rimmed.

"The doctor was here an hour ago to check on you, but I should call him back now that you are awake," she said, mostly to herself. Then, she turned back to me. "Are you all right? Feeling better? Does anything hurt?"

Everything hurt, but I didn't want to tell her that. My mother could overreact well enough on her own without my help.

"I'm all right," I said, pressing a palm to my forehead. Bending my elbow hurt, but nothing was excruciating. "What happened?"

I knew what happened to some extent, but I didn't know if she knew what happened.

"A handyman at the theatre heard you scream and found you lying on the floor unconscious." She pressed a hand to her chest and closed her eyes. "I can't even imagine what you were doing up there, but he said it looked like you'd fallen from the rafters. You had a large bump on your head that they think happened when the flashlight fell from your hands and hit you in the head. Does any of that sound familiar?"

I nodded. "A little bit."

I had fallen and a flashlight had definitely hit me on the head, though none of it happened quite the way they suspected.

I could still feel the cool fingers wrapped around my ankle.

I'd been attacked.

"What were you doing up there?" she asked. I could tell by the disappointed look on her face that she had already guessed at what I was doing. She sighed. "Alice. What happened to that actor was an accident. The paper reported on it. There is nothing else to be found."

I had more reason than ever to know that was not true. Someone had tried to hurt me, perhaps even kill me, because they believed I was close to solving the case.

Why would they do that if they weren't guilty of Phineas St. Clair's murder?

Still, I didn't want to worry my mother. I also didn't want her to know Mr. Williamson himself had asked me to investigate the case. He had enough on his plate dealing with his theatre and his romance with Lady Haddington that I didn't want to send my mother to his house in a rage. So, I stayed quiet and nodded, letting my mother think I agreed with her.

AFTER A FEW HOURS, I convinced my mother I was well enough to be alone, and she left. Hopefully to get some sleep. She'd only been gone a short while when a knock sounded on my door. It was the maid, Louise.

"A letter for you, Miss Alice," she said, holding out an envelope. Her eyebrow raise and barely contained smile told me the letter was from someone she was particularly fond of.

I thanked her and unfolded the stiff stationary.

Alice,

Are you well enough for visitors? Would you welcome me even if you were? I won't come until I know it won't distress you.

Sherborne

Sherborne Sharp would be waiting a long time, in that case. His letter hinted that he was worried about me, but I knew why he wanted to come. He had warned me over and over again not to get involved in this case. He'd tried to convince me to leave it to the police, but I hadn't listened. And now, I was lying in bed, covered in bruises, and nursing a damaged ego, as well.

I knew Sherborne Sharp well enough to know his visit would include a lethal dose of smugness. He wanted to tell me that he was right, and I was wrong, and I was in no mood to hear those words just yet. Perhaps ever.

I tucked the letter into the drawer of my bedside table and did my best to forget about it.

Just after lunch, a much more welcome visitor made an appearance. Louise announced Thomas' arrival, giving me time to tidy my hair and sit up in bed before he was shown into my room.

Under normal circumstances, Papa never would have allowed a man into my room, but since Mama was refusing to allow me to walk, though I felt perfectly capable, there was nowhere else for me to receive visitors.

Thomas looked nervous as he stepped inside, folding his hands behind his back and doing his best to keep his eyes from roaming around the room.

"How did you hear the news of my accident?" I asked.

"Everyone at the theatre is talking about it," he said. Then, he lowered his head, cheeks turning pink. "I hope I'm not intruding."

"No, of course not. I'm sorry, I should have started with that." I held out a hand for Thomas to grasp and lowered my head. "Thank you so much for coming to visit me in my crippled state."

Thomas smiled for a second before his face went

pale. He looked at my prone form under the bedding. "Crippled?"

"According to my mother," I teased. "Really, I'm fine. Just a few bruises."

His shoulders relaxed in clear relief, and then he frowned at the obvious bump on my head. His golden hair fell over his forehead as he bent to examine it. "Large bruises, by the looks of them."

"Do not get into an altercation with a metal flashlight. You will lose."

He smiled. "Noted."

I told him to sit in the chair next to my bed that my mother had dragged in from the library, and Thomas obeyed, folding his hands in his lap. He wanted to know what I remembered, but I stuck to the story I'd told my mother.

"Nothing?" he asked, obviously disappointed. "You really don't remember a thing?"

"The knock to my head must have shaken the memories right out." I shrugged. "I suppose it is a good thing I don't remember. If I fell as far as they think, it must have been frightening."

He frowned. "So, do you remember what you were doing at the theatre? You said once that you were there to support Mr. Williamson, but he was not the one to find you. You were alone when a handyman found you."

"The gossip at the theatre is very specific," I observed, a slight edge to my voice. I'd fielded questions from my mother and dodged Sherborne Sharp's critiques, but I did not expect such things from Thomas. Especially because we did not know one another particularly well. We'd only met a few days ago at the tour of the theatre.

And then we'd met there several times since.

I felt the beginnings of a thought forming in my mind, and I ignored whatever Thomas was saying to chase after it.

I'd only ever seen Thomas at the theatre. Even the day we were supposed to meet for the afternoon show, he'd been standing outside several hours early. Next to the group of reporters.

When I really thought about it, Thomas was full of questions. For me and Mr. Williamson. He also had more information than the general public about the crime itself. It had been Thomas who had told me about the thread found in Phineas' hair. How would he know anything about the findings of the coroner, especially since such information had not been made public?

The realization hit me all at once, and I gasped.

"What is it?" Thomas asked, leaning forward, laying a hand on my arm. "Are you all right, Alice? Is it something I said?"

"It is everything you've said." I pulled my arm out of his reach and angled my body towards him. He must have seen the coolness in my expression because he pulled away, putting distance between us.

"Alice?"

"What is your name?" I asked. "Who are you?"

"Thomas," he said. "I introduced myself to you the day we first met."

"On the tour. I remember," I said. "You told me you were Thomas, the son of a banker and a banker yourself. You claimed to be an aspiring actor."

Thomas shifted in his chair. "Why would that be distressing you now?"

"Because you're a liar."

He made no move to deny my claim, and my stomach dropped. I didn't want it to be true, but everything began making sense.

"You were with the pool of newspaper reporters the day I saw you outside the theatre," I said, my voice shaky. "When I told you I'd been invited by the owner of the theatre personally, you said, 'how lucky for me, then.'"

The memory made me feel sick.

"I thought it was because you liked me."

"I did," Thomas said. "I do."

I shook my head. "Then you would have told me the truth. You wouldn't have lied to me."

Thomas leaned forward, his elbows resting on his knees. "I had to lie, Alice. I couldn't tell anyone the truth."

"What is the truth?" I asked, wanting to hear it from him directly.

"You already know," he sighed.

"Say it."

Thomas sat back in the chair, sinking down in defeat. "I'm a journalist for a newspaper."

I'd already figured it out, but the words still pulled a disbelieving laugh out of me. I now remembered seeing his name printed beneath the article about Phineas St. Clair's death being an accident. Thomas Bailey. I couldn't believe it had taken me so long to put the pieces together.

"I know how you must feel about reporters," he said softly. "I remember when your family was in the paper constantly. I recognized you immediately, and I didn't intend to use you for information. But then you knew the owner of the theatre, and when Mr. Williamson wasn't allowing any reporters to come inside or to conduct interviews, you became my best chance at a scoop. So—"

"You used me," I finished for him. "You made me trust you and then used me to further your career."

"It sounds worse than it is when you phrase it like that."

"It sounds like the truth," I said, crossing my arms over my chest and looking away from him.

"Alice," Thomas said. "Please. I truly am your friend. I would have told you the truth eventually."

"Once I was no longer useful to you," I snapped.

Honestly, I didn't know Thomas well enough to feel betrayed. He didn't owe me anything. It wasn't as though we'd been lifelong friends. More than anything, I felt foolish. I should have suspected he was a reporter from the beginning, but I'd been so wrapped up in the case and my personal tension with Sherborne Sharp that I'd allowed myself to be blind to the truth.

"Perhaps you should go."

"Alice, please," Thomas started.

I held up a hand to silence him. "That was not a request. Please, leave."

Thomas hesitated, staring at the side of my face, silently begging me to meet his eyes. But I wouldn't. Phineas St. Clair had learned the hard way that he couldn't trust anyone, and I was determined not to make the same mistake. Thomas had proven himself a liar, and now I would distance myself from him for my own safety.

Finally, Thomas shuffled out of my room with a sigh and one last glance back to my bed. Once he was gone, I sagged down under the blankets and fought back tears. I couldn't trust anyone.

I couldn't tell my parents the truth, I couldn't trust Mr. Williamson with information about the case, and making new friends with the same blind naiveté with which I had always done was clearly no longer an option. I would have to face this alone.

I pulled the covers up to my chin and rolled to my side. The drawer where I'd tucked Sherborne's letter was half-open, allowing me a glimpse of the tan stationary inside. My fingers itched to pull it out and write to him. He knew the truth about my investigation. He knew me well enough to suspect I'd somehow involve myself in the happenings at the theatre. Sherborne Sharp was perhaps the only person in all of London who I could trust, and I was pushing him away.

With aching joints and a heavy heart, I pulled the blankets over my head and tried to sleep.

17

My mother checked on me several times throughout the night. It worried her when I didn't eat anything from the tray she'd sent up for dinner or for breakfast the next morning. And when I didn't ask to be allowed out of bed, she talked about sending for the doctor again. I knew she was nervous for me, but I couldn't muster the energy to try and ease her concerns. I was too preoccupied with feeling pitiful.

When my bedroom door opened for lunch that afternoon, however, I was determined to put on a brave face. I would eat something and try to push away the feeling that the world would cave in on me at any second.

Except, it wasn't my mother carrying the tray. It was Louise.

She smiled and set the tray on my bedside table. She looked so much like her cousin, Judith. They had the same red hair and pale skin. Though, Louise was tall and thin where Judith was rounder.

"How are you feeling this afternoon, Miss?"

"Fine," I said unconvincingly. "I'm hungry."

"Your mother will be happy to hear that. I've been instructed to stay here until you've eaten something."

"I'm sorry she left you such a boring task." I reached for the small bowl of soup and took a slurping bite. "There. Now you are free to go about the rest of your duties."

"Actually," Louise said, leaning in towards my bed. "I wondered whether you wouldn't like my company. I have some news."

"What sort of news?"

"About the theatre. And Judith. Would you still like to be kept informed about what is going on there?"

I'd asked Louise to keep me up to date if she should learn anything new about what was going on behind the scenes. Now, however, that Sherborne Sharp's theory that I was in over my head had been proven right, I wasn't certain I wanted to know anything. Maybe it would be best if I just let it all go.

I tried to convince myself, but the desire to know the truth burned too brightly to be ignored. Reluctantly, I nodded. "Yes, I'd like to know."

"Judith wants to leave the theatre group," Louise said, the information spewing out quickly. She took a calming breath and continued. "She used to boast about how fabulous her job was, but now, suddenly, she isn't content there. She came to ask me for help finding a position in a house here in London. Can you believe that?"

"No," I said, brow furrowed. "How did you learn this?"

"We had lunch yesterday," she said. "It was the first time I'd seen her face-to-face in over a year, and she did not look like a woman who worked a luxurious job. She was more battered and bruised than I am, and I work with my hands all day long."

I sat up, attention fully piqued. "Bruised?"

Louise nodded and gestured to her arms. "She had bruises across her arms, a few scratches, and her nails were chipped. She said it was from the endless hours hemming and sewing, but I've never seen a seamstress look like that. Apparently, the work they have her doing is quite grueling. And to think, I was jealous of her."

"To think," I said softly.

I'd never seen Judith with bruises before. Nor the head costumer. Nothing about Judith's appearance had seemed out of place at all when I'd seen her just moments before my accident. So, how had things changed so quickly in such a short amount of time?

"Something has definitely changed at the theatre," Louise said. "More than just the bruises, Judith had nothing but horrible things to say about Alfred Grey. For months, he was all I heard about. I wanted to know more about Phineas St. Clair, but Judith would send me letter after letter raving about how wonderful Alfred was. And now, she seemed repulsed by his very name."

"Did she say anything about him?"

"Just that he was the same as every actor she has ever met," Louise said. "My guess is that she doesn't like the way he is adapting to his role as the lead. All of my friends are talking about him now that he is the star of the play."

"Maybe Judith doesn't like not being his only admirer," I said aloud.

"Exactly," Louise said. She shrugged. "Either way,

now she is coming to me for advice, which is something I never thought would happen."

Louise didn't seem at all displeased by her cousin's sudden misfortune. In fact, she seemed to be enjoying it. I couldn't entirely blame her. Being the less successful daughter in my own family gave me an insight into what it would be like to be the less successful cousin. And Louise was certainly the type to enjoy being the one people would go to for advice and assistance.

While Louise was talking, I'd unknowingly eaten the entire bowl of soup and the hunk of bread there, and I felt bolstered. Not only by the food, but by the new evidence.

If Judith was suddenly bruised and ready to escape the theatre, one had to wonder what had changed for her in one short day. The only thing I could think of was my accident.

To my memory, I'd bounced off of several different surfaces during my fall, so it was quite possible I'd also hit my attacker on the way down. Perhaps, that could account for Judith's injuries. Also, if she had any fear of being found out as Phineas' killer, maybe she thought it would be best to try and silence me and then leave the theatre company altogether and start over as a maid. She might hope the attack would frighten me into silence so she could pretend the entire thing had never happened.

And as far as motive, her love of Alfred was reason enough. She adored the man and thought he deserved more time in the spotlight, so when her attempts to sabotage Phineas' costume did not work, she decided a physical attack would be better. Maybe she didn't know the light would kill him. Or maybe she did. Either way, she marked the spot with her red pencil, tied the light up with a bit of thread, and then waited until the right moment to drop it.

Maybe Alfred even knew about the plan. Maybe he was tired of assisting Phineas and was ready to be known for his own talent, so he let Judith take care of things. That would explain why they'd been huddled together, smiling, moments after the accident. It would also explain why Alfred had threatened me at Mr. Williamson's party and didn't want me to investigate the death. More than anything, however, this theory would explain why Judith was so distressed over Alfred's disinterest in her. She had risked everything to help him succeed, and he still didn't care about her.

Louise spoke for several more minutes about where she could get Judith some work and, sensing my disinterest, left as soon as I finished the food. I was so lost in thought I barely noticed.

MAMA AND PAPA were happy to see me eating, but my mother still wouldn't hear of me going any further than my own bedroom door.

"You are not strong enough for the stairs," she said. "Besides, that is why we have a household staff. They are here to help you."

"I am strong enough. Honestly." I turned to my father, eyes pleading.

"This is your mother's decision," he said, laying a

hand on her shoulder. He'd grumbled several times over the last day and a half that if I had been hurt anywhere else other than a friend's business, he would have been speaking with a lawyer. As it was, even he couldn't deny that Mr. Williamson was overwhelmed with everything on his plate right now and did not need a lawsuit adding to the pile.

I didn't want to make a fuss, anyway. I had all but begged Mr. Williamson to allow me access to the theatre, and he had grudgingly accepted. If it had been up to him, I would have been at home rather than climbing the stage rigging.

"It is my decision," my mother said, patting my leg under the comforter. "You need to rest for another day to be sure you are healing properly."

The only healing I had to do was to wait for the bruises to fade, but I knew there was no use explaining that to my mother, so I agreed with her and feigned exhaustion. She ushered my father out, insisting I needed my rest, and an hour later, I heard them close themselves in their own room. The moment they did, I slid out from under the covers, pulled on a walking skirt and matching coat, and made my way down the back staircase that led to the kitchen.

The kitchen was empty for the night, so no one saw me sneak out the back door and cross the garden to the old carriage house where the family car –and its driver – were housed. George answered on the third knock.

"I thought you were supposed to be resting," the chauffeur said, glancing up at the mostly dark house. "It is late."

"I need a ride," I said.

George asked surprisingly few questions, and within ten minutes, we were in the car and headed towards the theatre. He knew enough about current events to guess it had something to do with Phineas St. Clair's death, but much like the head costumer, George did not want to know any unnecessary information. It would only get him into trouble later. I was happy to grant that request.

"Wait for me here," I said. "I won't be long."

I left George at the curb as I raced up the steps to the theatre.

There had been a performance that night, but it had ended over an hour ago. The stairs, usually teeming with people and, for the last few days, reporters, were empty. I could see lights on through the glass front doors, but when I pulled on the handle, the door thudded in the frame. Locked.

I could have knocked, but if anyone answered, they wouldn't let in a strange girl from the public. But I also couldn't give up so easily. I walked around the front of the building and rounded the corner.

An alley ran behind the building. It was a place for trucks to pull in and unload equipment and scenery for the plays and performances. There were a few vehicles parked along the edge, but more importantly, the back door had been propped open.

I said a silent prayer of thanks for my luck and slipped inside.

I was at the end of the long hallway of dressing rooms, right next to the costume department. The light inside was off, the costumer and Judith gone, and I passed by without slowing down. If I did run into anyone,

I needed to look like I belonged. I needed to get to the stage.

When I was halfway down the hallway, a black clad member of the backstage crew walked out of a room, but he turned in the opposite direction without looking my way. I made it to the stage without being seen.

Unlike with the dent in the floorboards after Phineas' accident, there was no physical proof that I had been attacked backstage. The steep stairs to the lights were unscathed, and even the thin piece of dented wood I'd slid beneath the curtains was still in the exact place where I'd left it. It was almost as if it hadn't happened at all.

Except, it had happened. I'd been attacked, and I wanted to know why.

There was every possibility that any thread or other evidence left behind by the killer was gone now, but I wouldn't be able to rest until I'd climbed the rigging once more and checked for myself.

This time, there was a light in the back of the stage that had been left on. It shined directly down on where the actors would stand, but it was enough light to see by. If there was anything to find, I would be able to find it. So, I began to climb.

When I reached the point in the stairs when I'd been violently pulled back to the ground, my body froze up. Just for a second. Then, I kept going. I climbed until I was able to pull myself up onto the landing and plant my feet firmly on the wooden platform.

I absorbed the moment for a second, proud of myself for overcoming the fear, and then I walked out across the bridge that spanned the two sides of the stage.

It seemed silly to risk so much for a single thread, but it was the one piece that would pull my theory together. Without it, I had accusations, but no proof. With it, I could go to the police and tell them with confidence that Phineas' death had been orchestrated, even if I couldn't say with absolute certainty who had done it. Pointing them in the direction of Judith and Alfred Grey would likely answer quite a few questions, though.

I knelt down on the bridge and gripped the edge of the wood, anchoring myself. Then, I leaned down and ran my fingers along the bar where the light that had fallen had been anchored.

I expected to have to hunt and search for the thread. Honestly, I half-expected not to find anything at all. However, the moment I began to look, I felt a whisper of movement against my fingertips. I grabbed at it and there it was. The brown thread.

I tugged on the string, but it didn't move. I leaned further until I could see under the board slightly, and I could see that the string was looped around a bolt on the underside of the bridge. It was looped around the bolt with one side stretching towards the light and the other side hanging down half a meter towards the stage floor below. It had been cut short, but if it had been full length, I could imagine it hanging down in perfect reach of someone standing in the wings of the stage.

That was all I needed to see. If I went to the police now and got them to the theatre immediately, they would find the thread and realize that it matched the scrap piece found in Phineas' hair. They would have to come to the conclusion that someone had rigged the light and when the string was pulled to release the light, it had torn and a piece had fallen onto the dead man himself. It was a horrible possibility, but there seemed to be no other reason why a string would be tied in the rafters in such a way. It was the only thing that made sense.

I didn't want to tamper with the evidence, so I dropped the string and stood carefully to my feet. My parents would be angry when they found out I'd left the house, but when the police reopened the case and arrested the murderer or murderers, they would have to forgive me.

I'd walked back to the landing and was about to descend the steps when I realized, someone was climbing them.

I hadn't heard anyone coming. No squeak of floorboards or rustle of fabric to reveal them. If I hadn't turned around when I had, I never would have seen them coming.

"Hello?" I called, my voice shakier than I liked. "Who is that?"

The person made no move to announce themselves, and I could feel my blood go cold. I had to get down. I had to escape.

With the stairs blocked, the only way out would be on the other side of the stage. I crossed the bridge quickly but carefully, and sighed in relief when I safely reached the other landing. As I did, however, I looked back over my shoulder and realized the person climbing the stairs had mounted them. They were standing on the landing opposite me, dressed entirely in black, still silent as a ghost.

"Who are you?" I asked. "Why are you doing this?"

The person stood there in the shadows for a second,

letting my fear build, and then they reached up and pulled back their dark hood.

Alfred Grey looked across the bridge at me, his eyes narrowed in anger, his jaw set. "You couldn't let this go, could you?"

18

"Help!" The dark curtains around me swallowed my voice, making it sound small and meek, even though I was screaming with all of my might. "Help me!"

"There is no one else here," Alfred said. "I made sure of it. And as far as anyone else knows, I'm back at the hotel. I exited through the fire escape so no one would see me in the lobby. I'll re-enter that way to secure my alibi. No one will ever know I was here."

"Why would you need an alibi?"

Alfred tipped his head to the side, and his thin face split into a comically wide grin. "We both know you are a clever girl, Miss Beckingham. Don't feign ignorance now."

I nodded in silent agreement. Clearly, the time for performing was over. We were being honest with one another now.

"You attacked me yesterday."

Alfred nodded. "And yet, you returned. I suppose I

underestimated you. I thought the frightening experience would be enough to keep you away, but apparently you can't be discouraged so easily."

"You killed Phineas St. Clair." This was a new revelation to me, one I had only become certain of when Alfred pulled back his hood.

Again, he nodded. "No one else suspected anything. If they did, they had more sense than you. They stayed quiet."

"Why?"

He groaned and rolled his head back on his shoulders. "Once again, we both know you are a clever girl. You figured it out, after all."

In a way I had. I knew Phineas had been killed to benefit Alfred, but I was prepared to pin the deed on Judith. The evidence pointed back to the costume department, and Judith had been ready to run from the theatre, so I'd made an assumption. Eventually, the trail would have led from her to Alfred, but I hadn't quite gotten there yet.

"You wanted to be the star," I said. "You were tired of sharing the stage."

"No," Alfred said, taking a step forward. The entire rigging moved slightly. It was sturdy, but the vibration still made me flinch. "I was tired of being shoved aside by a broke, desperate man who was clinging to stardom. Phineas wouldn't give up a single show because he needed the money. He spent all of his time on stage or chasing after rich widows for table scraps, yet he was the one everyone cared about. He was the man every woman wanted to be with. He was the actor getting five-star reviews written in papers around the country."

"You were jealous."

Alfred's face went red. "I was angry. Rightfully so."

He was violent and threatened, and if I pushed him too far, he would push me from the rafters. Of that, I had no doubt. I needed to keep him talking long enough to back my way towards the stairs, descend them, and run from the theatre.

Even then, there was no guarantee of escape. If we were truly alone in the building like Alfred said, he could beat me down the stairs and kill me on the stage below just as easily.

I remembered the feeling of his cold hand wrapping around my ankle. His hand had been cold when I'd shaken it at the party. I hadn't made the connection. If I didn't play this right, those cold hands could be around my neck soon enough.

"How did you do it?" I asked.

The corners of his mouth turned up in a smile. "How do you think I did it?"

"Thread from the costume department and some kind of pulley system."

Slowly, Alfred lifted his hands and clapped as though I were a performer. "It was so dark backstage that no one saw the cord hanging there. I was able to leave it until the moment I needed it. When the scene happened, I grabbed the string and waited for Phineas to hit his mark. As soon as he did, I pulled on the string. It tore on a metal edge of the light and brought the whole thing down. I wasn't sure it would kill him, though I didn't mind. Either way, I would get my time on stage."

His confession was cold, calculating. It made me feel sick.

"Honestly, I hoped the police would catch on. I'd left a trail of clues leading back to Judith in case I was found out. She was in love with me and, if questioned, I would have told them she'd been obsessed with me. I would have told them how Judith had Phineas' wardrobe altered so I could have more stage time and when that didn't work, she went into a frenzy."

"You would have framed her?"

"Certainly," he said without hesitation. "I would do what needed to be done to ensure the plan worked."

"You're a monster," I said, the words slipping from me. I'd intended to keep him talking, to keep him calm so I could escape, but he was so callous that I couldn't stop myself.

"I didn't kill Rosalie," Alfred said, as though that somehow exonerated him of any wrongdoing. "I changed the scene with Phineas so she would be safe. A monster wouldn't do that."

The change in the script. I'd seen it on Phineas' pages the day I'd gone into his dressing room. In the previous version, Rosalie's character hugged his and clung to him desperately, but in the new version, Phineas pushed Rosalie away. That had all been part of Alfred's plan.

"A monster would hit a girl over the head with a flashlight to keep her quiet."

Alfred sighed. "That was necessary. You were going to expose my crime. Besides, as I've already mentioned, I could have killed you, but I didn't."

"Should I thank you?" I spat.

"Yes, actually," Alfred yelled, growing suddenly angry. "I would have let you live if you'd only stayed away. I warned you at the party, and you didn't listen.

So, when I saw you leave Rosalie Stuart's room, I knew you required more than a threat, and a little tumble down the stairs wouldn't kill you. But even that wasn't enough. Here you are again, forcing me to take yet another life."

"No one is forcing you to do anything, Alfred."

"What is my other option?" he asked, stepping forward onto the bridge. The rig shook again, and I instinctively took a step back. My heel was against the lip. I couldn't go any further or I'd fall backwards, but I didn't feel confident in my ability to spin around and get down the stairs quickly in such a tight space. Alfred could cross the bridge and get to me while I was still in reach. A fall from this high would leave me winded, giving him time to climb down to me.

My heartrate began to quicken and my palms grew sweaty, which was not helping the situation. I was trapped.

"Should I give up the fame I've worked so hard for and go to prison?" he asked. "Should I waste my talent behind bars? I don't think so. Not for you or Phineas St. Clair. Not for anyone. I've worked hard to get where I am, and I won't allow a curious girl to ruin it all for me."

"I won't tell," I said breathlessly. "Let me go, and I won't breathe a word."

Alfred lowered his head and looked at me from beneath heavy brows. "We both know that is a lie."

"They'll suspect a crime if a second person dies in the theatre in the same week. The police will reopen the case."

"And blame Judith," he said easily. "As for you, you've already fallen from the rafters once. Who is to say the amateur detective didn't climb up here again and slip? It will be a tragedy but not anyone's fault."

He was right. On both accounts. Judith would be blamed if anyone was blamed at all, and my death would be an accident. Sherborne would regret not trying to stop me, my parents would have to lose a second child, and Mr. Williamson's theatre would close. Everything would be ruined because I had to solve a case.

A wave of despair like I'd never experienced before washed over me, and I was overwhelmed by it. So overwhelmed I didn't notice Alfred walking towards me until he was halfway across the bridge.

He picked his way across the wooden platform carefully, moving with measured, menacing steps.

The cloud of despair was still lifting when I realized there was another figure on the rigging with us. Only this figure was not hidden in shadow or dark clothes. It was Judith.

My eyes went wide, and she lifted a finger to her lips, urging me to stay quiet.

Just like I hadn't heard or felt Alfred climbing up the stairs, I hadn't heard Judith, either. She ascended the stairs silently, and was moving steadily towards Alfred. Perhaps, if he'd been standing still, he would have felt her coming. As it was, he was too busy stalking towards me to realize a threat was creeping up behind him.

"Wait," I said, holding out a hand when he was little more than an arm's length away.

"No time to wait," he sighed, annoyed. "I'm ready for this to be over."

"So am I."

Judith's voice obviously surprised Alfred. There was

just enough time for his mouth to fall open and his eyes to go wide before Judith grabbed his shoulders and shoved him sideways.

He plunged over the edge.

Seconds later, we heard him hit the stage below with a heavy thud.

Judith and I rushed down the stairs to see him sprawled across the stage, where he made no attempt to get up. He was still lying motionless on the floor as we escaped the building and went in search of help.

19

Mr. Williamson held up the newspaper as soon as I walked through his office door the next evening.

"You did it."

I smiled and closed the door behind me. "I see you read the paper."

"Everyone has," he said. "How could they not? This is the story of the year. The decade, even!"

"Not quite." Though, I'd been forced to turn down four different vendors selling papers on the corners. Phineas St. Clair's death being reversed from an accident to murder was the best scoop any journalist could ever hope for.

"'*Phineas St. Clair Murdered, Understudy Arrested*'," Mr. Williamson said, reading the headline.

I knew for a fact Thomas Bailey's name was under the headline. Someone had found his address and had her chauffeur slip a letter outlining the details of the case under his front door, though I would never admit to it.

"I don't know who his anonymous source is, and I don't care. I'm just glad my good name has been restored." Mr. Williamson dropped the paper on his desk and leaned back in his chair, his arms folded behind his head. "How are your parents feeling about it all? Your father was not pleased with me for bringing you on as a private detective, but I'm sure you've talked to him by now."

"I have. They are both still disapproving, but coming around to the idea." Truly, I had given my parents little choice. I understood their anger came from fierce love and protectiveness, but I also would not be held captive in my bedroom, and I explained as much to them. I hinted at the possibility of my moving away from the family home, and they instantly became much more accommodating.

"Good," Mr. Williamson said with a clap. "Because you did excellent work. I wish there was some way I could repay you. As I've explained, the theatre is still going through a difficult time financially, but I suspect business will be up in the future."

"I do not want your money, but there is some way you could repay me."

"Oh?" He raised his brows. "Whatever you want, Miss Beckingham. I am indebted to you."

I pivoted away from his desk and paced across the room and back again. When I was standing in front of him again, I held out my hand, palm upwards. "I would like my mother's bracelet back."

Mr. Williamson's smile slipped, he blinked at me, stunned. Then, his cheeks went red. "What do you mean by that?"

"I overheard you describe the snake watch Lady Haddington had given to Phineas St. Clair before his death—the one that had been stolen from his room—and I didn't put it together right away. I thought maybe you'd stolen the watch, because how else would you have known of the watch's design? But stealing a gift from a dead man's dressing room hardly makes one a thief. What was Mr. St. Clair going to do with such a gaudy watch, anyway?"

Mr. Williamson shifted in his chair, his face going from red to white as the blood drained from it.

"Then, reports of thefts kept popping up, and they went far beyond the scope of this week. Women were losing purses and jewelry, and my own mother lost her favorite bracelet the night we came to the theatre for that fateful performance. Perhaps, if you hadn't mentioned the theatre's financial troubles to me, I wouldn't have pieced it together, but you did, and I did. So, I would like the bracelet back."

"Alice," Mr. Williamson said, shaking his head. "That is a serious accusation."

"It is, and I am not making it lightly. I saw you steal from Sherborne Sharp in the lobby of the theatre, though I didn't realize it at the time." Mr. Williamson had sandwiched Sherborne's hand between his own, and I only realized later that he was removing Sherborne's watch. As a former thief himself, I was surprised Sherborne didn't catch the trick.

Mr. Williamson opened his mouth like he wanted to argue, but then he shook his head, pushed away from his desk, and opened the top left drawer. Inside was a stash of jewelry. He plucked my mother's bracelet out from the bunch easily.

"Would you like Mr. Sharp's watch?"

I shook my head. "Life has a way of giving each of us what we deserve. I suspect that was Sherborne's come-uppance."

He closed the drawer and hung his head. "Will you tell everyone? The theatre is finally being viewed in a good light again and now it will all be ruined."

"I won't say anything," I said.

Mr. Williamson snapped his attention up to me. "You won't?"

"If the thefts stop now, then I'll stay quiet."

"They will," he said quickly. "I assure you."

"I know you were desperate, and you probably did things you are not proud of, but there is hope for you yet, Mr. Williamson. There is time to become a better man."

After all, I'd seen it done before. I'd met Sherborne Sharp in the shadows of my mother's room, rifling through her jewelry, and now he was a good friend.

"And if you don't," I added on my way out the door, the bracelet tucked into my coat pocket. "I have a reporter friend at a local paper who would love the inside scoop."

Mr. Williamson's mouth pinched together in a straight line, and I left him that way, with a word of encouragement and a somber warning.

THE SKY HAD BECOME overcast since I'd gone inside. The sun had sunk below the horizon, drenching everything in a shade of gray, and I pulled my coat tightly around me to fight away the chill.

The other night, after my terrifying encounter with Alfred Grey, I had sent George to Thomas Bailey's house and then straight home as soon as Judith and I had spoken to the police. I did not want my parents to know he was the one responsible for driving me to the theatre that night. Even though I'd asked him to, there was a chance they would never forgive him.

I'd done my best to keep my distance from the chauffeur since then, but I wished I'd asked for a ride this evening. My fingers felt numb with cold and it had grown dark outside sooner than I thought it would.

I felt the first prickle along the back of my spine when I was walking out of the theatre, but I ignored it. When it happened again a block later, however, I turned around.

There was a figure. A manly figure leaning against a light post, one leg crossed over the other as though he'd been standing there a long time, though I didn't remember passing him. He had only recently moved to stand there.

I turned away and kept walking, trying to ignore the sinking feeling in my stomach. It was probably a lingering uneasiness left over from my near miss with Alfred Grey the night before.

When the tingle moved down my spine yet again, I spun around, and this time, the man had peeled himself from the light post and was walking behind me.

My heart rate quickened, and I turned from side to side, ready to make an escape should I need to. But just before I could dart off the sidewalk and flag down a passing car for help, the figure lifted their head, and I saw the face of Sherborne Sharp smiling at me.

"You are lucky I haven't hit you with my purse yet," I said, pressing a palm to my chest. "Creeping behind women in the shadows like that is not at all gentleman-like."

"Who ever said I was a gentleman?" he asked, his voice smooth and deep.

"You did. Several times."

"Oh, my mistake." He smiled at me, and it was warm and familiar, and for the first time in what felt like weeks, I smiled back.

"Are you here to gloat?"

"Never. I am a gentleman, after all." He laughed at my eye roll and then grew serious. "I came because I have information for you."

"I've already solved the case, so your warnings are just a waste of breath at this point."

"It is not about that," he said. "I heard you loud and clear. Our relationship is rooted in business, and I come bearing the information you asked me to uncover."

He delivered the line in such a flat, emotionless way. Entirely different from the way he'd been talking moments before. Was that what I could expect from a business relationship with Sherborne Sharp? If so, I was not interested. I would rather endure his nervous hovering.

"About that," I said. "I was upset at the time and over-whelmed with the case. I did not intend for my words to come off so harshly or to hurt you in any way, and I apologize."

Sherborne tipped his head to the side. "Are you saying you would like to be my friend, Alice?"

"I did not say that."

He lowered his chin to his chest, his smile devious. "Are you admitting that you miss me?"

"I certainly did not say that either," I said louder, though my smile was hard to fight.

"Good," he said, lifting his head and straightening his shoulders. "Because that would be very unprofessional of you."

I frowned at him for a moment, and he glared back, a wink his only sign that he was teasing.

"Now that that is settled, what do you have to say?" I was eager to move on to the matter at hand, not only because I wanted to know what information he had uncovered, but also because we'd stepped into unfamiliar territory for a moment there.

Sherborne opened his mouth to speak, but before he could say a single word, a female voice shot out from the gloom behind him. We both turned just as Judith separated from the fog.

"I'm so glad I caught you," she said.

I wanted to wave her away and keep talking to Sherborne, but he tipped his head to me and left before I could beg him to stay.

"Sorry if I interrupted something," she said, looking curiously after Sherborne.

"You didn't," I lied. "He was already leaving. Did you need something?"

"Just to thank you," she said. "Things became very busy after...well, after everything that happened, and I didn't get the chance to thank you for solving the crime. If you hadn't, I would have gone on thinking Alfred Grey was worthy of my affection."

"I should be the one thanking you, Judith. Without you, I'd be—"

"Don't say it," she said, pressing a hand to her chest. "I can't bear the thought of what he would have done to you. It is too horrible."

"I won't say it, but thank you all the same."

She waved away my apology. "I saw Alfred leaving the hotel by the fire escape and I trailed him to find out why he was being so furtive. At the theatre, when I saw him following you up those stairs, I suddenly realized what he meant to do to you and what he had already done to Phineas. Of course, I had to stop him," she explained.

"I see. So, what will you do now?" I asked. "Louise mentioned you might go into service as something like a housemaid."

Judith shrugged. "Perhaps eventually, but for right now, I'm going to go home. It has been too long since I've seen my family, and I miss them."

"That sounds lovely."

"It will be," she said with a smile. "I need to be around ordinary people. I'm done rubbing elbows with the rich and famous for now...maybe forever."

Judith told me to send her love to her cousin because she would be leaving town before she could stop in to see Louise, and then we hugged and parted as friends.

~

I KEPT an eye out for Sherborne my entire way home, but he never reappeared. When I walked up the steps to my house, however, I saw a note pinned to the door.

A,

I'll meet you at the corner tomorrow at 1.

-S

I desperately wanted to know what information Sherborne had uncovered about The Chess Master right now, but it would have to wait. And maybe it was for the best. I was still coming to terms with the facts of Phineas St. Clair's murder and my altercation with his killer, so perhaps another night of sleep would do me well. It would give me another twelve hours to close the chapter on the theatre murder and prepare myself to reopen the chapter on Edward's death.

For years, his death had haunted me. First, because it was a terrible loss of the brother I'd thought I'd known. And then, because of the mystery I realized was surrounding it.

That night, as I lay in bed with my blankets pulled up to my chin, I stared at the ceiling and wondered if this time tomorrow I would have the answers I'd been hoping for. I wondered if I would finally know who had killed my brother and why.

~

Continue following the mysterious adventures of Alice
Beckingham in
"Murder in the Early Hours."

ABOUT THE AUTHOR

Blythe Baker is the lead writer behind several popular historical and paranormal mystery series. When Blythe isn't buried under clues, suspects, and motives, she's acting as chauffeur to her children and head groomer to her household of beloved pets. She enjoys walking her dog, lounging in her backyard hammock, and fiddling with graphic design. She also likes binge-watching mystery shows on TV.

To learn more about Blythe, visit her website and sign up for her newsletter at www.blythebaker.com

Made in the USA
Coppell, TX
06 August 2020